DEATH FROM THE SKIES

Geronimo raised his hand over his eyes and squinted. "What are those things attached to the bottom of its wings?"

"Your guess is as good as mine," Blade said, and saw the aircraft arc into the heavens again. As it did, a small spherical object dropped from the right wing directly toward them. Blade's intuition flared, and he gave his friends a shove. "Into the forest! Move!"

Confused, Geronimo and Hickok nonetheless trusted the giant's judgment enough to obey him instantly and without question. They darted to the northwest.

Blade raced on their heels, his gray eyes glued to the spherical object. When it was 15 feet from the soil, he threw himself to the ground and bellowed, "Get down!"

Again the pair complied, and not a moment too soon. For when they hit the ground, a blast with the force of a quarter-ton of dynamite rent the air and rocked the ground . . . .

Other titles in the *Endworld* series:

1: THE FOX RUN
2: THIEF RIVER FALLS RUN
3: TWIN CITIES RUN
4: THE KALISPELL RUN
5: DAKOTA RUN
6: CITADEL RUN
7: ARMAGEDDON RUN
8: DENVER RUN
9: CAPITAL RUN
#10: NEW YORK RUN
#11: LIBERTY RUN
#12: HOUSTON RUN
#13: ANAHEIM RUN
#14: SEATTLE RUN
#15: NEVADA RUN
#16: MIAMI RUN
#17: ATLANTA RUN
#18: MEMPHIS RUN
#19: CINCINNATI RUN
#20: DALLAS RUN
#21: BOSTON RUN
#22: GREEN BAY RUN
#23: YELLOWSTONE RUN
#24: NEW ORLEANS RUN
#25: SPARTAN RUN

ENDWORLD

#26: MADMAN RUN

DAVID ROBBINS

LEISURE BOOKS NEW YORK CITY

Dedicated to . . .
Judy, Joshua, and Shane.
To everyone who remembers
those scary Saturday afternoon matinees.

Oh. And to the memory of
H.G. Wells. His imagination
has inspired so many.

A LEISURE BOOK®

June 1991

Published by

Dorchester Publishing Co., Inc.
276 Fifth Avenue
New York, NY 10001

Printed in the United States of America.

Dear Plato:

Hi.

Enclosed is the file you requested. I had to go into the basement to find it. No one has read this particular one in many years, and I was extremely surprised when you asked for it.

Although you are probably as familiar with the facts as I am, I thought it might help to refresh both our memories and provide some background.

All three of them were in their midteens at the time. Blade had just turned 16, according to the records. This was the fourth of their little adventures and the one that affected Blade the most.

As usual, I employed a subjective style instead of an objective narrative. History should be vibrant, not dull.

Knowing you as well as I do, I took the liberty of going through the archives for the other files related to Blade's travels during the same period. If you desire to see them, I'll be happy to send them over.

By the way, does Blade know you're doing this? He doesn't take kindly to anyone prying into his past without a good reason. I know the files are official records open to every Family member, but it's a privilege that should not be abused, even by our esteemed leader.

Does this have anything to do with the recent incident involving Blade's son Gabe and that mutated black bear? If so, I understand your motive. Will you give this to Blade before or after you read it? Heh-heh.

Well, I've rambled enough. Stop by and visit me sometime. I get lonely with no one to talk to.

Respectfully,

RLD

The Chronicler

CHAPTER ONE

The scorching July sun was perched at its zenith above the northern Minnesota landscape. A slight breeze provided scant relief from the heat, occasionally stirring a leaf in the verdant forest. Birds sang gaily and insects buzzed, indicating there were no predators abroad.

Three youths were hiking to the southeast at a brisk pace, despite the temperature. All three carried backpacks, and all three were armed to the proverbial teeth.

In the lead walked a teenager whose features revealed his Indian ancestry. The blood of the Blackfeet flowed in his veins, and perhaps it was due to his biological inheritance that he had always excelled at hunting and trapping. He wore torn jeans and a faded blue T-shirt that fit his stocky frame snugly. Tucked under his brown leather belt were two tomahawks, one on either hip. He held a Winchester 30-30 in his left hand.

"Whose bright idea was this, anyway?" he asked while swatting a fly the size of his thumb.

"It wasn't mine, pard," replied the second youth in line. His hair was blond, and a thin moustache just beginning to take shape on his upper lip was the same color. He wore buckskins that served to accent his alert blue eyes. Strapped around his slim waist were a pair of Colt Python .357 Magnum revolvers sporting pearl handles. "Blame this on Mikey."

"The new name is Blade, remember?" stated the third member of their party, a giant standing six-feet eight-inches tall and endowed with a herculean physique. A black leather vest and jeans scarcely contained his bulging muscles. Around his waist were two matched Bowie knives, while slung over his left shoulder was a Marlin 45-70. His hair was dark, his eyes a penetrating shade of gray.

"Well, excuse me for living," the blond gunman said. "I've been calling you Mikey since we were knee-high to a grasshopper. Just because you had your Naming last week doesn't mean I'll automatically stop."

"You will if you know what's good for you," Blade declared.

The gunman halted and turned. "Was that a threat?"

"It was a promise," the giant said.

"Oh, brother. Here we go again," the Indian interjected, looking at the gunman. "Hickok, he's right and you know it. You don't like us to call you Nathan any more, so have the decency to call Mikey by his new name." He grinned broadly.

"I reckon you have a point, Lone Elk," Hickok said. "Too bad your Naming isn't for a couple of months yet. Have you picked the one you want?"

"I've decided to take the name Geronimo."

The young gunfighted cackled. "Leave it to you to pick the name of a bloodthirsty Injun. Why couldn't you select something civilized?"

Lone Elk straightened indignantly. "Like what, for instance?"

"Oh, I don't know. How about Percival or Barney?"

"If they're such great names, why didn't you pick one

for yourself?''

''Because I like a handle with class.''

''You know what you can do with your class.''

Hickok pretended to be offended. ''Why are you being so touchy? It was the Founder who said a person's name should reflect their personality. I can't help it if you're more the Percival type than a Geronimo.'' He glanced at the giant. ''What do you think, Mikey?''

''Leave me out of this,'' Blade responded. He walked past them and took the lead, refusing to become embroiled in yet another senseless argument over their names. Although the three of them were the best of friends, they still found plenty to bicker about, especially after they'd been hiking for miles through dense woodland in 100 plus degree weather.

Blade was proud of his new name. He'd spent countless hours narrowing down a list of those he liked the most and had finally chosen the one that best described his outlook on life and his preference in weapons. Ever since the age of four or five, he'd entertained a fascination with edged arms of every type, and over the years he'd become extremely proficient in the use of all the knives, swords and daggers in the huge Family armory. So it was only natural for him to take a name that typified his passion.

The way he saw it, he owed a debt of gratitude to the long-deceased Founder of the Home, Kurt Carpenter, the man who had constructed the 30-acre survivalist retreat in northwestern Minnesota shortly before the outbreak of World War III. A wealthy film maker who realized the inevitability of nuclear conflict after the liberal Russian president was deposed by militant hard-liners, Carpenter had spent millions on his pet project. It was he who first dubbed the compound the Home and designated his select band of followers as the Family, and for 92 years they'd survived in a world deranged by radioactive and chemical toxins.

Carpenter had instituted many unique social reforms

designed to stabilize the new society, and among them was the ceremony known as the Naming. Because he had worried that subsequent generations would lose sight of their historical roots, he'd encouraged all parents to have their children search through history books and choose the name of any historical personage they admired as their very own, a name they were formally christened with on their 16th birthday. The practice was later changed to allow those undergoing such a special event to select the name from any source they liked or even to adopt one of their own devising, as Blade had done.

The young giant suddenly halted and cocked his head. He belatedly realized that all the birds and insects were quiet, which could only mean trouble. Unslinging his Marlin, he surveyed the forest but saw nothing to arouse alarm.

Hickok and Lone Elk were 20 feet away, still going at it.

Blade shrugged and continued trekking in the direction he hoped to find the castle mentioned in the Founder's diary. Carpenter had meticulously noted every item of interest in a daily log, and one of those items talked about a mysterious castle belonging to an eccentric recluse who lived 15 miles from the Home. The cryptic reference had aroused Blade's curiosity, and he'd persuaded his friends to do a little exploring with him to see if the castle still stood.

"Hey, Mikey!" the gunfighter yelled. "Wait for us."

Halting, Blade turned and regarded them critically as they jogged up to him. "This isn't the time or place for your petty squabbles," he said.

"Whoa! Who died and made you boss?" Hickok quipped.

"As you pointed out, this was my brainstorm. So by rights I should take charge," Blade noted.

"We're both Warriors. I don't see why you should lord it over us just because you had an idea for once."

"What about me?" Lone Elk interjected. "I can lead, too."

Hickok snorted. "You don't count. You're not even a Warrior yet."

"But I will be soon," Lone Elk pointed out.

Blade smiled. "I bet you can hardly wait."

"You don't know the half of it."

But Blade did have an excellent idea of the excitement his friend felt. After all, he'd felt the very same way when it came time for the Family Elders to decide on his nomination.

The Warrior class consisted of twelve Family members who were carefully screened not only for their ability as fighters, but for their temperament and intelligence as well. They were diligently trained under the tutelage of a retired Warrior in everything from the martial arts to combat psychology. Because of a recent mishap, three vacancies had developed. Blade and Hickok had applied and were accepted, and shortly it would be Lone Elk's turn.

"If you ask me, we don't need someone in charge," Lone Elk stated. "It's not like we're on official Family business. All we're doing is taking a day to goof off."

"Speak for yourself, twinkle-toes," Hickok responded. "I'm a Warrior now. I never goof off."

Lone Elk unexpectedly leaned down and inspected the grass at their feet.

"What the blazes are you doing?" Hickok demanded.

"Making a note of this spot. I want to return next week and see how well you've fertilized it."

Blade chuckled and marched onward, eager to reach their destination. If they didn't spot the castle soon, they'd have to head back to avoid being abroad after dark—not that they were afraid—but at night the predators and mutations were out in force, and anyone foolish enough to roam around courted death or risked being maimed.

The eerie stillness persisted. Not so much as a bee buzzed.

"Have you guys noticed how quiet it is?" Blade asked.

"Yeah. And I don't like it," Lone Elk said.

"What's the big deal?" Hickok wanted to know. "We'll blow away anything stupid enough to mess with us." His hands hovered near his Pythons.

Lone Elk stopped. "Did you hear that?"

"I didn't hear nothing," Hickok said. "Your mind is playin' tricks on you."

As if deliberately trying to prove the gunfighter wrong, howls and snarls erupted from a dense thicket to the west, and a moment later a feral pack of mutations burst from cover and charged.

CHAPTER TWO

They resembled coyotes in shape and size, but there any resemblance ended. Hideously transformed by an unknown agent, the nine creatures loping toward the three humans lived purely to kill. Their bodies were hairless and covered with sores that oozed a yellowish-green pus. Their teeth were bared, their eyes blazing like miniature beacons of blood-crazed insanity.

Blade had seen such horrors before. The Family referred to such creatures as mutates. None of the Elders knew what caused them to exist, although Blade's father and another man who was called Plato had often speculated the chemical weapons employed during the war were somehow responsible. If radiation was the culprit, so the reasoning went, then there would be humans similarly affected, and there wasn't a single report in the entire Family history of a human mutate. As far as anyone knew, only reptiles, amphibians and mammals were mysteriously altered. Never had anyone observed a mutated bird or insect. Since the war, the mutate population had grown dramatically to the point where they were a serious threat to all travelers, day or night. Plato, the wisest member of the Family, believed the mutates were increasing by geometric progression, and he was eager to secure a live juvenile specimen for analysis. Unfortunately, the only way to get one was to kill it.

The young giant pressed the Marlin to his right shoulder, sighted on the foremost mutate, and fired.

Struck in the head, the lead coyote was flipped backwards by the impact of the slug. Other members of the pack collided with it, causing momentary confusion.

Lone Elk opened up with the Winchester, levering off two shots in rapid succession, the sharp retorts producing two dead beasts.

Leaving six.

Blade was aiming at another onrushing form when Hickok moved around him. He held his fire, the Marlin still raised to provide cover if need be, but as he anticipated, his help wasn't required.

The blond youth's hands streaked those gleaming Colts from their holsters and twin shots sounded as one. Three times the gunman stroked each hammer, and after the six shots there were six twitching, dying mutates stretched out on the grass. Each one had been shot in the head between the eyes. Dead center between the eyes. Grinning, Hickok ambled toward the pack, ready to finish off any that tried to rise. None did.

Lone Elk glanced at Blade and said softly, "If he gets any faster he'll have to change his name to lightning." Then he looked at the gunman and declared, "You could have saved some for us."

"I can't help it if you're as slow as molasses," Hickok retorted, in the act of prodding each coyote with a toe.

"Don't get smart with us, ding-a-ling. We know your secret," Lone Elk said.

"What secret?"

"Your so-called quick draw is a trick done with mirrors."

"Anytime you feel inclined to try and outdraw my mirrors, feel free to let me know."

Lone Elk stepped forward to help check the bodies. "You'd shoot little ol' me?" he asked innocently.

"Of course not. Oh, I might crease your head, but it's so swelled up you'd never notice the difference."

Blade surveyed the woods in case there were more mutates in hiding. Nothing moved, and he relaxed a bit. "We'd better get going," he urged. "If there are scavengers in the area, they're bound to have heard the shots."

Hickok looked up and smirked. "There you go again, trying to take charge."

"You can't blame him," Lone Elk said. "It's in his veins. His dad is our Leader, after all."

"And one day Mikey might follow in daddy's footsteps," the gunfighter joked.

"I have no intention of becoming the Leader of the Family," Blade asserted stiffly. "How many times do I have to tell you?"

"You can tell us until you're blue in the face, pard, but we won't believe you."

"Why not?"

"Because we know you," Hickok said. Satisfied the mutates were all dead, he began to reload the Magnums.

"And what does that mean?" Blade demanded.

"It means you're a rotten liar. Deep down you really do want to become Leader some day."

"You're nuts."

"Hey, Lone Elk agrees with me," Hickok said, glancing at the Blackfoot. "Don't you?"

"Are you talking to me?" Lone Elk rejoined.

"No, I'm talkin' to one of the blamed critters," the gunman muttered, then raised his voice. "Of course I'm talkin' to you, mutton head."

"If you care to address me, from now on you'll call me by my new name."

"You want me to call you Geronimo?"

"Yes.'"

Hickok paused, a cartridge in his left hand. "But you haven't had your Naming yet."

"So? I will, soon. And since Mike and you already have your new names, I want you to call me by mine."

"Forget it, dimwit."

"What harm can calling me by my new name do, yo-yo?"

"Technically you don't have a new name until after the ceremony, and I aim to abide by the rules until then."

"Suit yourself, Nathan," the stocky teen said, using the name bestowed on the gunman by his parents, and walked off.

"Of all the childish antics," Hickok protested. He swung toward the giant. "What do you say?"

"I say we humor him. If he wants to be called Geronimo, it's fine with me."

"Some attitude for a future Leader."

"If you keep bringing that up, you won't have a future," Blade chided and followed Geronimo.

Hickok trailed after them, still reloading. "Well, don't expect me to break the rules. As far as I'm concerned, Lone Elk is Lone Elk until the Naming is over."

"Do whatever you think is best," Blade said.

"Besides, I still figure he'd make a better Percival."

They traveled another mile and neared a hill with a bald crown. A hawk soared on the air currents to their right, and a pair of deer fled at their approach.

"I sure do like the outdoors," Hickok remarked, his thumbs hooked in his gunbelt. "Don't you, Lone Elk?"

There was no answer.

"You're serious about not talkin' to me, aren't you?" Hickok inquired.

There was still no answer.

"Fine. Suit yourself. See if I ever speak to you again."

Blade grinned and stared at the crest. It would be a good spot to take a break and decide whether to continue or turn back. The heat was getting to him, and he wouldn't mind heading for the Home with their goal unaccomplished. Once back, he could take a refreshing dip in the moat.

Minutes later they stepped from the trees and halted just below the rim.

"Let's rest a bit," Blade proposed.

"Sure, fearless Leader, whatever you want," Hickok said, sitting down on a log. He studiously refrained from gazing at Geronimo.

"I'd like to take a vote. Do we head on or head home?" Blade asked them.

"It makes no difference to me," Geronimo said.

"I couldn't care less," Hickok added.

"So the decision is mine," Blade declared and moved toward the top of the hill for a view of the country beyond. If there was no sign of the castle, he'd return to the compound. Perhaps, after consulting the Founder's diary once more and pinpointing the exact location, he might try to find it again one day—on a cooler day.

"Hey!" Geronimo suddenly yelled. "What's that?"

Blade spun and saw his friend pointing skyward. He tilted his neck and spied something flying far overhead. At first he thought it was a hawk, until the glint of sunlight off a metallic surface demonstrated otherwise.

"It's not a bird," Hickok stated, rising.

"The thing appears to be made of metal," Geronimo mentioned.

Stunned, Blade watched the object perform a tight circle hundreds of feet above them. Could it be an airplane? he wondered. Thinking of all the books dealing with aviation in the Family library and all the plane photographs he'd admired, he decided the object was far too small to be an aircraft.

"I hear a strange buzzing," Geronimo announced.

Blade heard the sound, too, as if a million angry hornets were in flight en masse, and his brow knit in bewilderment.

"Maybe we should try to shoot it down," Hickok suggested.

"Why? It's not trying to harm us," Blade replied. "Unless it attacks, we leave it alone."

"Yes, *sir.*"

The alien device swooped lower, revealing its shape.

With a start, Blade realized he'd been wrong. He distinguished a set of long, thin wings and the unmistakable contours of a tail assembly; he realized it was a plane, but the smallest one he'd ever seen. One of the books he'd read came to mind, a volume detailing how to construct and operate tiny aircraft known as model planes. If he wasn't mistaken, the thing in the sky was a model plane. But it couldn't be.

"It looks like a baby plane," Hickok noted, apparently having the same train of thought as Blade.

"Such things don't exist any more," Geronimo said.

"Peepers don't lie," Hickok stated.

Buzzing even louder, the diminutive aircraft angled to the southeast and flew off.

Eager to see where it went, Blade hastened to the top of the hill and stared after it. His gaze strayed to the valley below and every fiber of his being tingled at the sight of the structures less than half a mile off. "Bingo," he said. "We've hit the jackpot."

Hickok and Geronimo were on the crest in seconds.

"It's the castle!" the gunman exclaimed.

"Or what's left of it," Geronimo amended.

From a distance, the castle appeared to be in a severe state of disrepair. Windows were missing. One of the four turrents was damaged. Vines grew in profusion up the slate gray walls. A flock of starlings was flying above it, bearing eastward.

"I vote we check the place out," Blade said.

"Count me in," Geronimo agreed.

Hickok nodded. "I've always wanted to see a real castle."

The three of them hastened down the far side of the hill into yet more forest, revitalized by their discovery.

Blade took the point, selecting the easiest route, by-passing the thickest brush and skirting clusters of large boulders. After traversing 50 feet, he looked at the ground and halted in astonishment.

Hickok almost bumped into the giant. "What the heck did you stop for?"

"This," Blade said, indicating a well-worn trail leading deeper into the valley. The path wound past them to the northwest.

"So you found a game trail. Big deal."

"Take a closer look," Blade advised.

The gunfighter squatted and peered at a strip of bare earth, his eyes widening when he recognized the distinct impression of a shoe. "Someone has used this trail recently."

"Within the past day or two," Geronimo said.

"Stay alert," Blade instructed them. They followed the path until they arrived at the border of a spacious meadow. Blade stopped short again, shocked by the unexpected.

Corn, wheat, oats and other crops covered the eastern half of the meadow, aligned in separate plots. From the hill, the meadow had been partly obscured by the trees, and the crops tended to blend into the surrounding vegetation. No one would ever suspect the land had been tilled unless they came right up on it.

"Someone lives in this valley," Hickok said.

"In the castle," Geronimo speculated.

"There's enough there to feed a hundred people," Blade noted. "Maybe we've stumbled on a pocket of survivors."

"Let's hope they're friendly," Hickok stated.

Blade led them across the meadow. Halfway to the other

side ther trail broadened, becoming a grassy road. Ruts formed by heavy wagon wheels lined the soil, and there were many more footprints in the intermittent bare spots. Except these prints were of naked feet.

"What do you make of it, pard?" Hickok asked when they halted to examine the tracks.

"Beats me," Blade said. He glanced at Geronimo, who was kneeling and lightly touching the impressions. "You're the tracking expert. What can you tell us?"

"It's hard to determine precise numbers because so many have passed by, but I'd guess that ten to twenty people use this road on a regular basis, at least once a day. And the freshest wagon ruts were made this morning."

"This morning?" Blade repeated, scanning the meadow. "Then they must still be close by." He had the oddest feeling that the three of them were being watched, but by whom was anyone's guess.

"We'd be smart to take cover," Hickok suggested.

"No. If we did, these people might get the wrong idea and think we're here to harm them. We'll stay out in the open and demonstrate they have nothing to be afraid of."

"And what if they're the ones who want to harm us?"

"We'll cross that bridge when we come to it."

The gunman sighed. "Don't take this personal, but you're too trusting sometimes. Not everyone is as kind and decent as the folks at the Home."

Suddenly, from the woods to the south, arose harsh, mocking laughter.

CHAPTER THREE

Blade and his friends crouched and swung to the south, probing the trees for movement. After a minute Geronimo spoke.

"There's no one there."

"Go double-check," Blade said.

The youthful Blackfoot glanced at the giant, then nodded. "Whatever you want." He was up and off in a flash, weaving as he ran, the Winchester at the ready.

"Givin' orders just comes naturally to you, doesn't it?" Hickok asked.

"Don't start," Blade warned. "Someone has to check, and he's more skilled at moving stealthily than the two of us combined."

"Speak for yourself. Geronimo's good, but he has a long way to go before he's in the same class as Atilla."

Blade said nothing, his eyes on the forest. Attila was the current head of the Warriors, an extremely popular, extremely deadly man whose mastery of the martial arts, marksmanship and combat tactics bordered on perfection. His partisans believed he was the best Warrior the Family ever produced, a sentiment Blade shared.

Geronimo had disappeared, melting into the foliage without disturbing a leaf.

"That hombre better be careful," Hickok commented.

"Do I detect a note of concern?"

"Me worried about that no-account Injun? Don't make me laugh."

"Why don't you just admit you love him like a brother?" Blade asked without taking his gaze from the woods.

"Sure I care about him. I care about you, too. But that doesn't mean I'll get all misty eyed if he gets himself killed. I just don't want him to lose the rifle, is all."

"Uh-huh."

"Don't you believe me?"

"In a word, no."

Hickok made a hissing noise. "You're gettin' real sarcastic in your young age, you know that?"

"Think so?"

"I know so. You're changing, Blade. You're not the carefree kid you used to be"

"Are any of us?" Blade responded. "And thanks."

"For what?"

"For calling me Blade instead of Mikey. If you don't stop, I'm liable to lose control and haul off and bust you in the chops."

"Sarcastic *and* mean. I liked you better when your main interest in life was catchin' crayfish."

"We all have to grow up sooner or later. Back in the old days, before the Big Blast, some people went through their whole lives without acquiring an ounce of maturity. It's not the same now. We don't have that luxury."

"You've been listening to Plato again, haven't you?"

"What's wrong with listening to the wisest philospher in our entire history? Even my dad looks up to him. Hearing Plato speak is like having the mysteries of the universe unraveled right before your eyes."

"Oh, brother."

Blade was about to elaborate when he saw Geronimo returning on the double.

"Find anythiung?"

"I didn't see anyone," Geronimo reported, "but I found a network of trails and a garden."

"A what?" Hickok asked.

Geronimo looked at Blade. "Kindly remind that know-it-all that I'm not talking to him until he calls me by my name or the earth plunges into the sun. Whichever occurs first."

Hickok glared. "Enough is enough, already. Come on, Geronimo, give me a break."

In two swift strides Geronimo reached the gunman and gave his startled chum a bear hug, actually lifting Hickok off the ground. "You did it! You called me by my new name!"

"It slipped out," Hickok exclaimed, flustered by the embrace. "Now put me down, you cow chip, before somebody sees us!"

Geronimo let go and beamed. "I knew you wouldn't let me down. For a White Eyes, you're not half bad."

"Yeah, well, let's not get all mushy about this. Show us the garden."

Nodding happily, Geronimo led them down the road through a narrow tract of woodland to a cleared area where flowers grew in profusion, neatly arranged in trimmed rows. There were roses, columbines, geraniums, violets, marigolds and more.

Hickok shook his head in astonishment. "I never would've believed it if I hadn't seen this with my own eyes."

"There must be someone living in the castle," Geronimo reiterated. "As far as I know, there aren't any towns nearby."

Blade thought of the laugh they'd heard and nodded. "Let's go see." He led them along the road, which wound past the garden, through yet another strip of forest, and angled directly at the castle.

The farther they went, the more obvious the damage became. The glass panes in those windows still intact were all cracked or splintered. Inch-wide cracks marred those sections of the outer wall where the vines had yet to get a purchase. And two other turrets were missing portions of their sides.

"I don't get it," Hickok said as they crossed a narrow field toward the medieval edifice looming in front of them. "Why are the crops and the garden so well taken care of, but the castle hasn't been fixed up in ages?"

Blade was wondering the same thing. He spied a wide wooden door at the base of the building. "We'll ask the owner."

When they arrived at the closed door, a raven perched on the battlements vented a strident cry and flapped into the sky.

"I'll do the honors," Geronimo offered, and knocked loudly. His blows seemed to echo within, then fade.

A minute elapsed, and no one acknowledged the pounding.

"Let me," Hickok said, delivering several firm kicks to the bottom panel.

Again there was no response.

"Maybe no one is in," Geronimo stated.

Blade grabbed a large black handle and tugged, but the portal refused to budge. "It's locked."

"Kick it in," Hickok suggested.

"Be serious."

"I am."

"No," Blade declared. "I told you we must make a good impression on these people, and we won't if we barge into their home."

"Then what do we do? Twiddle our thumbs until someone shows up?"

The giant bore to the right. "No, let's have a look around." He craned his neck to view the top of the castle as he walked slowly to the corner. If he didn't know better, he'd swear the place was uninhabited. But how could that be when the garden and the crops indicated there were occupants?

Around the corner lay more of the same, more vines and a cleared space between the structure and the trees. The lowest windows were all a good 20 feet from the ground, too high to reach without a ladder.

"This dump is sort of spooky," Hickok remarked.

"Don't tell me *you're* afraid?" Geronimo asked.

"No. I'm just bringin' up a fact is all."

Blade was halfway to the rear when he happened to glance at the grass near his feet. Lying within inches of his black combat boots was an apple core. "Look at this," he said and squatted.

The others moved in for a better glimpse.

"An animal, you think?" Hickok speculated.

"No," Geronimo said. "Animals eat cores. They don't care about ingesting a few seeds."

Blade jerked his thumb at the battlement. "My guess is that someone ate the apple up there and tossed the core over the side."

"I wish to blazes they'd show themselves," the gunman stated gruffly. "I don't like playin' cat and mouse, particularly when I'm the mouse."

Rising, Blade continued to the far corner. When he strode into the open, he couldn't quite credit the sight he beheld.

"Will you look at those!" Hickok marveled.

"What in the world are they?" Geronimo asked.

There were six small buildings situated in the middle of the yard, three in one row, three in another. Constructed from polished marble, they were one story in height and approximately 20 feet wide. They were ornately embellished with miniature columns and intricate engravings depicting elaborate scenes.

Blade scratched his chin, reflecting. He'd seen photographs of such buildings, but he couldn't recall where.

"They're too dinky to be houses," Hickok commented.

"Maybe they are memorials of some sort," Geronimo guessed.

An image flashed into Blade's mind, a picture in a book dealing with twentieth century social conventions and customs. "They're mausoleums," he informed his friends.

"Mauzi-what?" Hickok responded.

"Mausoleums. Places where the rich and famous were buried."

"Why would anyone want to be buried in a small house?"

"That was the custom before the war. Most people were buried in public cemeteries, and tombstones were placed over their graves. But those with money to spend could have a lasting monument erected in their honor."

"And I thought Geronimo has a swelled head."

Blade walked forward. "Loved ones visited regularly and deposited flowers in remembrance of those who died. Caretakers performed regular maintenance and upkeep to keep the tombs in top condition."

"I'll never understand the bozos who lived back then," Hickok said. "What good is buildin' a monument if you won't be around to enjoy it?"

They halted at the first mausoleum and studied the etchings. One scene displayed naked young men and women engaged in leaping over bulls by grabbing the horns and executing acrobatic flips.

"What the dickens is that supposed to be?" the gunman inquired.

"I believe it shows the bullfighters of ancient Crete,"

Blade surmised. "Don't you remember our classes on the subject?"

Hickok snorted. "I remember the paintings of the soldiers marching off to war or in battle, but I never paid much attention to those other pictures and drawings of men wearin' dresses and women in their birthday suits prancin' around trees."

"What a warped mind," Geronimo cracked.

The gunfighter disregarded the gibe. "Why would anyone want Cretan bullfighters on their tomb?"

Blade shrugged. "Maybe to show they were students of ancient history."

"Or to prove they were idiots," Hickok amended.

The giant moved to the recessed door and tried to open it, without success.

"You're not plannin' to go in there?" Hickok declared.

"I'm curious to see what's inside."

"I can tell you. An old wooden coffin and a bunch of moldy bones. Let's leave well enough alone."

Blade walked to the next tomb, which was slightly bigger than the rest, and stared at a pecular crest engraved near the top: A man in a suit of armor was holding the body of a child in one hand and the head in another.

"Disgusting," Geronimo said.

"Let me guess," Hickok stated. "This guy was tryin' to show that he was fond of the Middle Ages."

"Makes no sense to me," Blade chimbed in.

Geronimo dropped to one knee and ran his fingers over the grass. "This is strange."

"What is?" Blade prompted.

"A lot of people have been here within the past day or two."

"Standin' in front of this tomb?" Hickok said skeptically.

"No," Geronimo answered. "Going *into* the tomb."

Blade and the gunfighter exchanged bewildered expressions.

"You're crazy, pard," Hickok said.

"Which one of us is the tracker here? I know what I'm talking about. At least ten, possibly fifteen people entered this mausoleum."

"Did they come out again?" Blade asked.

"It's difficult to tell. Either they went in first and came out, or they came out, then went in."

"You must be sufferin' from heatstroke, pard."

Blade walked to the next tomb, thoroughly confused by the string of events. What connection was there between the tiny plane, the tilled plots, the apple core and the mausoleums? What was the significance of the laugh? And how did it all tie together with the castle?

He thought about the Founder's cryptic diary entry. Carpenter mentioned taking a hike and bumping into the castle's owner, a man named Edward, who had requested that he leave the estate at once. Although Carpenter tried to be friendly, the owner became angry and even threatened to club him with a walking stick. Rather than provoke the man further, Carpenter returned to the compound.

Blade realized the descendants of the recluse had been on their own for almost a century, completely cut off from the outside world. Perhaps they were simply afraid to make contact. He was more determined than ever to find them and convince them they had nothing to fear. If he practiced a little diplomacy, as his father was always stressing he should do, then he might persuade them to accompany him to the Home. The Family would be delighted at learning there were people living within walking distance, and friendly relations could be established. The Tillers would be very interested in learning the techniques these people used to grow such fine crops and flowers, and perhaps a system of trade could be set up.

The giant idly glanced at the castle and felt a prickling sensation run along his spine.

There was someone at one of the windows, staring back.

CHAPTER FOUR

She stood behind a shadowed pane crisscrossed with cracks, a vague, slim figure attired in what appeared to be a flowing white dress. Raven tresses cascaded over her shoulders. Unfortunately, the murky interior shrouded her facial features.

"Look!" Blade exclaimed.

Hickok and Geronimo spun, the gunfighter starting to go for his guns until he saw the reason for the cry. "It's a woman!" he blurted.

"What was your first clue?" Geronimo asked.

Suddenly, her white dress flowing, the phantom disappeared to the right.

"We've got to get inside," Blade said and ran to the rear wall. He scrutinized the vines, then reached out and tugged on one to test it. "These might hold our weight."

"Might?" Geronimo said, glancing at the nearest window.

"Let's give it a try," Blade said, slinging the Marlin over his shoulder and jumping with outstretched arms. He grabbed a stout vine and held on fast. "Let me go first. If the vines support me, we know they'll support the two of you.''

''Good point,'' Hickok said. ''You have been gettin' a mite big in the breadbasket.''

''I'm all muscle, and you know it,'' Blade stated, commencing the ascent. ''Keep me covered.''

The gunman stared at the windows and the battlement, ready to fire at the slightest hint of a threat.

''At least now we know there's someone home,'' Geronimo noted. ''I wonder who she is.''

''The tooth fairy,'' Hickok quipped and stiffened at a loud crackling and snapping noise from above. He took one look and tackled Geronimo, bearing both of them backwards.

''What the . . . !'' Geronimo declared.

Blade fell onto the ground, his powerful legs braced for the impact, and stumbled a few feet before he caught himself. ''The vines won't hold,'' he informed them.

''No foolin','' Hickok said, rising to his knees. ''You could have yelled or something. We were almost squished into pancakes.''

''Sorry. It all happened so fast.''

Geronimo stood. ''No harm done.''

The giant regarded the window, scowling, and walked to the right. ''We'll keep searching until we find a way in.''

''And what if we don't?'' Geronimo inquired.

''Then I vote we stay here overnight and try again in the morning.''

The gunman snickered. ''*Now* you want to have a democracy, huh?''

''What do you guys say?''

''If you want to stay, it's fine with me,'' Geronimo said.

''Good,'' Blade stated. ''I'd really like to get to the bottom of this.''

''Where you guys go, I go,'' Hickok said. ''Count me in.''

They rounded the southeast corner, passing a compact jumble of vines, and worked their way back to the front entrance without discovering a means of getting in.

"Now what?" Hickok asked.

"We'll patrol the ground, then make camp," Blade answered.

"I have a better idea. There are a lot of big trees in these woods. Why don't we chop one down and use it as a battering ram?" the gunfighter submitted.

"How many times must I tell you that we're not going to damage the property?"

"Listen to you. You're the one who said we shouldn't go bargin' in on them, and yet you were all set to climb up to a window just because you saw a pretty woman."

"I have no way of knowing whether she was pretty or not," Blade responded.

"Listen," Geronimo interrupted.

"What is it?"

"The little plane."

Sure enough, Blade heard the unmistakable buzzing of the tiny aircraft and peered skyward to observe it flying in a wide circle above the castle.

"A woman in white, some horse's butt who likes to laugh to himself, tombs decorated with space cadets who fought bulls for a living, and a midget plane." Hickok listed their finds. "This is too weird for words."

"It beats fishing in the moat," Blade said. "Besides, look at the bright side. Except for the mutates, we haven't been in any danger."

"There's plenty of daylight left, pard."

Blade headed toward the trees, intending to prowl the area, and was halfway there when the buzzing grew in volume. He gazed upward and saw the plane sweeping toward him. Amused rather than disturbed, he watched the craft dive closer and closer, puzzled by its performance. What purpose did it serve? Was someone foolishly attempting to drive them off using such a toy?

"Can I plug that contraption?" Hickok requested. "It annoys me."

"No."

Geronimo raised his hand over his eyes and squinted. "What are those small things attached to the bottom of its wings?"

"Your guess is as good as mine," Blade said, as he saw the aircraft arc into the heavens again. As it did, a small spherical object dropped from the right wing directly toward them. Blade's intuition flared, and he gave his friends a shove. "Into the forest! Move!"

Confused, Geronimo and Hickok nonetheless trusted the giant's judgment enough to obey him instantly and without question. They darted to the northwest.

Blade raced on their heels, his gray eyes glued to the spherical object. When it was 15 feet from the soil, he threw himself to the ground and bellowed, "Get down!"

Again the pair complied, and not a moment too soon. For when they hit the ground, a blast with the force of a quarter-stick of dynamite rent the air and rocked the ground, sending a shower of dirt upward like an erupting geyser.

Blade was on his feet and running for the trees before the thunderous detonation died away. Clods of earth rained onto his head and shoulders. He glanced around for Hickok and Geronimo, but both were lost in the grimy cloud.

The miniature plane droned somewhere overhead.

Unslinging the rifle, Blade gazed upward, hoping for a shot. He emerged from the dust into the bright light, spied the aircraft off to the right, and snapped the stock to his shoulder.

Its wings tilting, the plane abruptly banked and flew toward the castle.

Blade tracked the craft, tempted to try even though the odds of hitting it were miniscule. In frustration he lowered the Marlin just as two hacking forms hurtled into the open.

"Where's the plane?" Hickok asked, his hands on the Colts.

"That way," Blade disclosed, pointing. "Follow me." Wheeling, he jogged into the woods and took shelter behind a trunk.

"What the dickens did that thing drop?" the gunfighter asked, halting next to an oak.

"A bomb of some sort," Geronimo said.

"A couple of feet difference and we would have been goners."

"I had no idea planes that size could do such a thing," Blade observed. "How did it know exactly when to release the bomb?"

"Someone must be controlling it," Geronimo said.

"Whoever it is, they're worm food when I catch up with them," Hickok vowed.

Blade didn't argue. Whoever lived in the castle clearly wanted them dead. By all rights he should hasten to the Home and report the incident to Attila. But he was a Warrior now, and it wasn't fitting for a Warrior to let someone else do his fighting. If he wanted to be worthy of the distinction bestowed on him by the Elders, he must prove their judgment to be sound.

Then there was another angle to consider. If the three of them departed, whoever lived in the castle would be free to conduct unwarranted attacks on others who might wander by. Because of the castle's remote location, such a likelihood was remote. He couldn't ignore the possibility, though, and still uphold his pledge to safeguard human lives.

"So what now, fearless leader?" Hickok inquired.

"We carry on as planned," Blade proposed. "First we'll scour the area, then make camp for the night far enough away to be safe."

"How far is that?" Geronimo asked.

Lacking a definite answer, Blade straightened and moved to the west, conducting a search of the forest. He didn't know what he was looking for, but he knew he'd recognize it when he saw it. When he bisected a well-worn trail, he nodded in satisfaction. There were many prints in the soft soil. "What do you make of these tracks, Geronimo?"

Again the Blackfoot youth examined the ground. "It's the same as before. Lots of footprints, most naked, indicating regular, daily travel." He paused. "Something else also uses this trail."

"An animal?"

"If it is, it's unlike any animal I know of. I'd say these belong to a mutation."

Blade stepped over to inspect the tracks in question, and one look sufficed to prove Geronimo correct. The tracks were immense, 15 inches long and five wide, and were further distinguished by having only three large, oval toes. From their depth in the soil, the creature must be extremely large.

"Imagine the size of that sucker," Hickok said.

"Let's hope we don't run into it," Blade commented.

"Makes no nevermind to me," the gunman responded. "I can always use a little target practice."

Turning to the lelft, Blade stuck with the trail, curious about where it might lead. He wasn't curious long. In no time at all the trail brought them to the edge of the yard, but from the west. He stayed in the trees and stared at the mausoleums, reflecting on their possible significance.

To the north, faint but distinct, was the buzzing of the tiny plane.

"It must still be huntin' for us," Hickok said.

"Let's keep looking around," Blade proposed and went deeper into the woods.

They hiked a mile to the west without finding anything of importance, then swung to the south, then east, and ultimately wound up back on the side of the castle in the forest near the flower garden. By then the sun hung above the horizon.

"We should think about where we want to make camp," Geronimo mentioned. "I don't want to be in the open if there are big mutations roaming this area at night."

"The only place we can hole up is the castle," Hickok said.

"We'll make a lean-to and build a fire," Blade suggested. "Even mutations are scared of flames."

"You hope, pard."

While Geronimo tended to gathering firewood, Blade and Hickok constructed a serviceable lean-to, positioning the open end to the east. Twilight had descended by the time they were done. Geronimo collected stones and formed a ring. Then he placed tinder he'd gathered earlier in the center and removed a flint from his right front pocket.

"Want me to do any huffin' and puffin'?" Hickok offered.

"No, thanks. I can manage."

Blade deposited his backpack inside the lean-to and opened the flap. Inside was ammunition, rope, an extra pair of pants, a whetstone for the Bowies, a canteen, and a brown leather pouch containing his food supply. He removed the canteen and several strips of dried venison.

In another minute Geronimo got the fire going, and all three of them sat around the blaze, munching contentedly.

"This ain't so bad," Hickok said. "At least I'm not pullin' guard duty.

"What's wrong with guard duty?" Blade asked.

"It's boring."

"You should take your responsibilities as a Warrior more seriously. Boring or not, guard duty is essential to the security of the Family."

"Lighten up, big guy. I'm not about to sleep on the job, but you have to admit walkin' the walls leaves a lot to be desired."

"I like guard duty."

"You would."

"What's your point?"

The gunfighter took a bite of jerky and grinned. "You're so gung-ho, you make Attila look like a goof-off."

"I'll let him know you said that when we get back."

Geronimo cleared his throat. "Say, did either of you happen to hear the latest rumor?"

"What now?" Blade asked. "The last stupid rumor was something to the effect that Plato had tried to talk my dad into sending an expedition out to discover what happened to the rest of the country after the Big Blast. I checked with my dad, and he said Plato did mention the idea but never formally submitted it to the Elders. Maybe one day he will."

"This latest rumor has nothing to do with Plato."

"What is it, pard?" Hickok asked casually.

The corners of Geronimo's mouth curved upward. "There's a story going around that a certain young lady has the hots for a certain young man."

Blade stopped chewing.

"Really?" Hickok said. "I haven't heard. Who's the woman?"

"She's not exactly a woman," Geronimo replied. "In fact, she's the same age as us."

"We don't want to hear it," Blade stated gruffly.

The gunfighter glanced in surprise at the giant. "Since when don't you like to hear juicy gossip? If my memory serves, you were the one who went out of his way to learn everything he could about Rikki-Tikki-Tavi and Tanya. Am I right or am I right?"

Blade gazed at the sky. "You're blowing everything way out of proportion, as usual."

The gunfighter laughed. "Am I?" He turned to Geronimo. "Ignore him. What's this latest gossip?"

"I was told that Jenny has fallen head over heels for a certain novice Warrior."

"Jenny?" Hickok snorted. "Some gossip. Everybody

knows she's warm for Blade's form."

The giant lost his interest in the heavens. "What do you mean everybody knows?"

"Everybody at the Home, that is. I can't vouch for the rest of the world."

Geronimo leaned foward. "Sure, everyone knows they're in love. But did you know Jenny wants to bind before the year is out?"

"Do tell," Hickok said, glancing at Blade. "You're a mite young to be gettin' hitched, aren't you?"

"Geronimo doesn't know what he's talking about," Blade declared testily, taking a bite of venison. In the process he accidentally bit his finger.

Hickok snickered. "Oh?"

"I heard the news from Betty, who heard it from Cathy," Geronimo said. "And we all know Cathy is one of Jenny's best friends. According to her, Jenny tried to talk our good buddy into tying the knot but he refused."

The gunman grinned at the giant. "This gets more and more interesting by the moment. Why don't you want to bind?"

"For the very reason you gave. We're too young to get married. Maybe in a few years, after I've established myself as a Warrior and Jenny has become a fully accredited Healer, we'll tie the knot. Marriage isn't a responsibility to be taken lightly."

"Sounds a lot like guard duty," Hickok said and cackled.

They ate in silence for a while. Stars blossomed in the firmament, and a full moon rose to the east. A cool breeze afforded refreshing relief from the day's heat.

"There's something I've wanted to bring up," Geronimo remarked at one point.

"It's not more gossip, I hope," Blade said coldly.

"No. It's about us. We've been best friends since we were in diapers. When we were kids, we adopted the motto of the Three Musketeers, remember? Well, I'd like to continue this way during our adult years.''

''Get to the point,'' Hickok said.

''Okay. After I become a Warrior, why don't we ask Blade's father for permission to form our own Triad?''

Blade sipped at his canteen. The idea had merit. Since the Warriors were divided into combat units of three men apiece anyway, why not indeed? ''I like the idea.''

''Me, too,'' Hickok said. ''It'll save me the trouble of havin' to break somebody new in to appreciating my refined sense of humor.''

Geronimo chortled. ''*You* have a sense of humor?''

''We would work well as a team,'' Blade stated. ''I'm sure my dad would agree, and there's no reason the Elders would object.''

''One for all, and all for one,'' Hickok said, grinning.

Geronimo suddenly stood and peered into the shadowy forest to the south. ''Do you hear that?''

The gunfighter groaned. ''Not again.''

Blade was about to say he didn't hear a sound, when from off in the distance there came the distinct sound of a large animal—or something else—crashing through the undergrowth. It took him a few seconds to realize the thing was coming directly toward them.

CHAPTER FIVE

Hickok stepped from under the lean-to and straightened. "It sounds like a friggin' elephant."

"How would you know what an elephant sounds like?" Geronimo asked.

"I listen to you snore at night."

The crashing ceased as abruptly as it began.

"Maybe it's movin' off," Hickok said hopefully.

"And maybe it's spotted our fire," Blade stated. He moved next to the gunman and levered a round into the Marlin's chamber.

"I'll go out there and see," Geronimo offered.

"Not on your life. We'll stick together."

Hickok nudged the Blackfoot. "Sentimental cuss, isn't he?"

Without warning, the crashing resumed, growing louder and louder. A thumping noise became audible, mingled in with the breaking of limbs and the rending of brush.

"What's that?" Hickok whispered.

"Footsteps," Geronimo answered. He rose and joined them, the Winchester at his shoulder.

Blade peered into the dark woods. Although he knew an unknown creature was bearing down on them, he involuntarily stiffened when he detected movement at the limits of his vision. The thing's bulk was tremendous; a great, hulking mass of a brute almost as wide as it was tall, it appeared to be over ten feet in height.

"Dear Spirit," Geronimo exclaimed softly.

Reddish eyes the size of apples glared at them, and a rumbling, sustained growl issued from its throat.

"If it attacks, go for the head," Hickok recommended.

"I'd rather run," Geronimo said.

Blade agreed. An almost palpable aura of evil radiated from the beast, even at that distance, chilling him to the core. He tried to convince himself the sensation was all in his head, but couldn't. The size alone staggered him. Because of his own prodigious build, he'd rarely encountered any menace larger than himself. This thing dwarfed them all. Up close, it would even dwarf him.

"You guys have the rifles," Hickok said. "Why don't one of you take a shot?"

"I don't want to make it mad," Geronimo replied.

"Be serious, pard."

"I am."

The creature moved to the east, its red eyes fixed on their camp, plowing through the vegetation as if there weren't any. When it was nearly out of sight it vented a ferocious roar that caused every insect and animal within a mile's radius to fall silent. Then it departed, the thump of its feet receding to the southeast and finally fading away.

Geronimo expelled a sigh of relief. "That was too close for comfort."

"Didn't faze me none," Hickok claimed. "I could've taken it down, easy."

"Dream on," Geronimo said.

"Piece of cake."

Blade stared at the last spot he'd seen the thing, troubled

by his reaction. Rarely had he known the feeling of genuine fear, but while watching the creature he'd felt just that, a fleeting instant of stark panic. He shook his head to clear his mind of his apprehension.

Hickok glanced at the giant. "Are you okay, pard?"

"Fine."

"You sure? You look a bit peaked."

"I'm fine," Blade repeated sternly. He sat down in the lean-to, relishing the warmth of the flames.

"Why didn't it come after us?" Geronimo asked.

"The fire, maybe," Hickok said.

"A thing that big?"

"Maybe one of us has bad breath."

"Speak for yourself."

Blade swallowed water from the canteen and wiped the back of his hand across his mouth. "Do you want to draw lots to see which one of us pulls the first shift?"

"I'll take the first watch, if you don't mind," Hickok said.

"I'll take the second," Geronimo chimed in.

"Leaving me the third," Blade stated. "Fine by me."

The gunfighter took a seat, and after a minute Geronimo did likewise.

"This trip of ours is turnin' into quite an adventure," Hickok remarked.

Blade chewed on more jerky, engrossed in thought. When he'd expressed an interest in staying overnight, he hadn't foreseen they might have to take on a monster. He'd fought his share of genetic abominations in his time, but never anything as immense as the brute they'd just seen. If they were getting in over their heads, wouldn't the wise course of action entail returning to the Home? Sure, he was a Warrior, but he was new at his trade and had a lot to learn. The same with Hickok. He scanned the forest and realized they were stuck there whether they liked it or not, at least until morning.

"We should check the tracks that thing made at first light," Geronimo advised. "It might be the creature responsible for those strange three-toed footprints."

"If that critter comes back, let's offer it some grub and try to train it," Hickok said, smirking. "If it cooperates, we'll have it kick in the castle door."

The conversation drifted from the monster to a discussion of certain girls at the Home, with Hickok and Geronimo debating their assets and attractiveness for over an hour. Blade rarely spoke. His eyes darted to the woods whenever a noise was heard, and he kept the fire going high.

"Well," Hickok said at length, "I suppose the two of you will want to turn in soon."

"I'm beat," Geronimo commented.

"I'm not," Blade fibbed. "I'll stay up a while yet."

Hickok laughed. "Don't worry. I won't let the boogeyman slit your throat while you sleep."

"Not funny," Blade said sternly.

"Lighten up, Mikey. I was only kiddin'."

The giant leaned toward the gunfighter, his flinty eyes mere slits. "This is the last time I'll tell you. Don't *ever* call me that name again."

Shock registered on Hickok's face. He glanced at Geronimo, who shrugged, then nodded at Blade. "Sure, big guy, whatever you want. I didn't mean to get your goat."

"No offense taken," Blade said, although his tone contradicted the statement. He crossed his arms and hunched against the lean-to, glowering into the fire.

Geronimo spread out on his back and draped his left arm over his eyes.

For a minute Hickok regarded the giant intently, then he took a position on the east side of the fire where he could see in all directions and not have their makeshift shelter obstruct his view.

Blade idly gnawed on his lower lip, annoyed at himself for losing his temper over a trifle. He had no reason to jump down the gunfighter's throat, and he attributed his lapse to a bad case of nerves after the incident involving the monster. To cover his chagrin, he thought about other subjects—his dad, his budding friendship with Plato, his feelings for Jenny, and his new duties as a Warrior.

He appreciated his good fortune in having his dad as the Leader, but he disliked the extra attention directed his way because of it. The Elders all expected great things out of him. Plato claimed he possessed the spark of greatness within. Their compliments, however, fell on skeptical ears. As far as he was concerned, the only exceptional quality he possessed was size, which in itself hardly indicated any outstanding potential. On top of that, his whole goal in life was to serve as a Warrior until he reached retirement age and could sit on the council of Elders. Hardly a career that would result in terrific accomplishments.

Blade reflected on the comments his friends made about Jenny and recalled her asking him to bind. To say the least, he'd been surprised. Sure, they cared for each other. But they were only 16, and in his estimation they weren't mature enough yet to assume the awesome responsibilities of husband and wife. Jenny disagreed. She felt they were mature enough, but since girls invariably matured faster than guys, she was justified in making such a claim. He felt bad about disappointing her, but he wasn't about to say yes until he was certain they were both ready.

An image of Attila filled his mind—tall, lean, attired in black leather pants and a wolf's hide shirt, hair hanging to the small of his back and lively green eyes. There was a man! Of all the Warriors, of all the people at the Home next to his dad and possibly Plato, Attila impressed Blade the most.

The head Warrior possessed a carefree attitude that Blade keenly admired. Attila never lost his cool and always took everything in stride. Blade wished he could be the same way, wished others would refer to him as a man who lived life to the fullest and never got bent out of shape. Instead, everyone who knew him well claimed he was moody, an introvert, in a good frame of mind one minute and troubled the next. Maybe they were right. Ever since the death of his mom he'd been changed inside.

Blade's eyeslids drooped. He heard Geronimo snoring softly and saw the gunfighter staring at the fire. "Hickok," he said sleepily.

"Yeah, pard?"

"Sorry."

"For what?"

"For getting on your case."

"Don't sweat it. We all get cranky now and then."

"I seldom see you cranky."

Hickok grinned. "That's because I've naturally got a downright sweet disposition."

"I suppose you do."

"Why don't you grab some shut-eye, Mi—," Hickok began and caught himself, "—Blade. Geronimo will wake you when it's your turn to tend the fire."

"Thanks. Don't mind if I do." Blade sank on his side and felt the warmth of the flames on his face. Contented and comfortable, he drifted into dreamland.

When next his eyes fluttered open, Blade had to think for a minute to recall where he was. He spied Geronimo near the fire now and Hickok lying to the left, sound asleep. Inhaling loudly, he pushed up on his elbows and yawned. "Is it my turn yet?"

"No," Geronimo replied. "I just took over from motormouth a short while ago."

"I can pull my stint now if you like."

"There's no need. Go back to sleep."

Sighing, Blade settled down again and watched the flickering tongues of orange and red dance and writhe.

"Say, Geronimo?"

"Yes?"

"Would you say I'm moody?"

"Only during a full moon."

"I'm serious."

"Now and then. No more than the rest of us."

"Hickok is hardly ever moody."

"There's a reason for that."

"Oh?"

"Nathan is the only man alive who has a vacuum between his ears."

"He's sharper than most."

"True, but if you ever tell him I said so, I'll deny every word."

Grinning, Blade let his mind lapse into a disjointed state where his thoughts came in spurts. Finally, slumber claimed him.

What was that strange noise?

Blade didn't know if he were awake or asleep. He lay there, his eyes shut, and listened, positive something out of the ordinary had brought him around. Cracking his lids, he gazed at Geronimo, who was dozing while sitting upright, then at Hickok, who slept as peacefully as a baby.

He must have imagined the whole thing.

Just as Blade closed his eyes he heard the sound again, a peculiar, airy titter. Puzzled, he raised his head a few inches and gazed into the forest, astounded to behold dozens of things—moving about at the very edge of the firelight.

The vague shapes were thin and tall. They flitted about in the woods, prancing from tree to tree, giggling lightly all the while. Their skin had a pale cast, as if reflecting the moonlight.

Blade saw one of the things start to approach the camp. He sat up, grabbing the Marlin, and shouted, "Geronimo! Look out!"

In the fleeting interval between the instant the giant uncoiled and his bellowed warning, the creatures in the woods abruptly vanished, seeming to fade to nothingness in the blink of an eye.

Geronimo leaped to his feet, startled, the Winchester in his hands. "What? Where?" he exclaimed, looking in all directions.

A split second later Hickok came to his feet, both Colts drawn and cocked, bewildered but ready to fight. "What the dickens is going on?" he demanded.

Flabbergasted, Blade stood and stepped into the open. "Didn't you see them, Geronimo?"

"See what?"

"Those things in the trees."

The Blackfoot surveyed their surroundings again. "I don't see anything."

"They were there a few seconds ago. Dozens of them."

"Of what?" Hickok asked.

"I don't know. They were sort of like wood nymphs or fairies," Blade explained, unable to think of a more precise description.

"Wood nymphs?" Geronimo repeated.

"Fairies?" Hickok said.

"Yeah. You know. They were flitting around in the trees and laughing," Blade elaborated.

Hickok and Geronimo locked eyes, then the gunfighter twirled his Colts into their holsters and chuckled. "We'd better have the dried venison checked when we get back to the Home. They must be adding a new ingredient to it nowadays."

"Don't you believe me?" Blade asked.

"You've got to admit your tale is a mite hard to swallow."

"I saw them, I tell you."

"We believe you believe you saw them," Geronimo said, "but that doesn't necessarily mean they were really there."

"I *saw* them," Blade stressed.

Hickok made a show of turning in a circle while whistling and calling out, "Oh, little fairies? Where are you? Come out, come out, wherever you are."

Geronimo cackled.

"When have I ever lied to you?" Blade demanded, peeved at their attitudes. "One of those things was coming right toward us when I shouted. Somehow, they all vanished."

"Somehow," Geronimo said. "Like into thin air?"

"Yes. Exactly."

"Oh, brother," Hickok mumbled, laying back down. "Monsters with glowing eyes. Flittin' fairies. What I said before still goes. This place is too weird for words."

"I'd never doubt either of you," Blade said.

"Now don't get all upset over a bunch of wood nymphs," Hickok responded. "If you say they were there, then I'll go along with it. But let's be realistic. Even if there are a horde of fairies out there, I doubt they pose a danger to us. I can't see Peter Pumpernickel and his gang jumpin' our buns, can you?"

"That's Pan, dope," Geronimo corrected him.

"Whatever." Hickok stretched and closed his eyes. "If it's all the same to you, I've got to catch up on my beauty sleep. But be sure and wake me if Leapin' Leroy and his Killer Leprechauns attack."

Blade scanned the woods again and again, hoping for a glimpse of the creatures to redeem himself. None showed.

"Why don't you crash?" Geronimo suggested. "I'll keep watch for the nymphs."

"I'm not sleepy now," Blade said.

"Why waste the time staying up and waiting for those things to come back?"

"I can't honestly say."

Exasperated, Blade went under the lean-to and lay on his stomach. He began to wonder if he'd really seen them himself. His friends had never doubted him before. Maybe, because of everything that had happened in the past 24 hours, his imagination was playing tricks with him. He rested his chin on his forehead and patiently waited for his turn to pull guard duty, determined to stay awake. But after a while, despite his best intentions, he fell asleep for the third time and dreamed of rabid leprechauns in fairy suits swooping out of the sky to rend him limb from limb.

CHAPTER SIX

Leapin' Leroy was in the act of impaling him on a silver butter knife when Blade felt someone shaking his shoulder and sat bolt upright. He automatically reached for the Marlin, blinking in confusion, and only relaxed when he saw Geronimo kneeling at his side, regarding him as one might a lunatic.

"It's just me. Are you okay?"

"Yeah. Sure." Blade swallowed and gazed at the woods. "Is it my turn?"

"Yep. Nothing stirred the rest of my shift."

"Good," Blade said, retrieving the rifle and sliding out. "Get some sleep."

"I wouldn't mind pulling double duty."

"I'm fine. But you two clowns are beginning to give me a complex."

"Sorry. But I've never seen you so rattled before. What's wrong?"

"Nothing," Blade snapped.

Shrugging, the Blackfoot placed the Winchester near his chest and lay down. "Wake us at dawn."

"You got it." Blade stepped to the east side of the fire and squatted, shivering in the brisk night air. He stuck the rifle in the crook of his arm, rubbed his hands together, and feeling his stomach growl, resolved to hunt game for breakfast. Fresh roasted meat might do them all some good.

Sitting, Blade scrutinized the heavens, marveling at the celestial spectacle. There seemed to be a well-nigh infinite number of stars, a sea of cosmic creation aswarm with fiery beacons radiating light and life to countless worlds. He wished he'd been born before the war, for the sole reason of being able to witness the historic missions to Mars and the establishment of a lunar base in a joint venture of the United States, the Soviet Union and France. It was most unfortunate space exploration ground to a halt after the liberal Russian president was deposed and the hard-liners regained control. America and Europe devoted all of their attention to producing armaments instead of spaceships.

The sputtering fire snapped Blade out of his contemplation. He realized they needed more wood. Slinging the Marlin over his right shoulder, he walked into the forest, scouring the ground for fallen limbs. He loaded his arms and returned.

As Blade bent to set the wood on the ground, a faint rustling arose to his rear. He pretended not to notice, straightened slowly, and whirled.

The ruse worked.

One of the things was back, standing near a tree 20 feet away, watching him.

Instantly Blade took off, not bothering to yell to his companions because they wouldn't believe him anyway. He needed proof, and the only way to obtain it was to capture the creature. His legs pumping, he covered the ground in prodiguious bounds consistent with his size. Only one other person in the entire Family had ever beaten him at a foot race—a martial artist named Rikki-Tikki-

Tavi—and he had no doubt he'd catch the nymph.

As quick as the giant was, the pale being was even quicker. It spun and took off like a frightened deer, moving with astonishing speed and seeming to fly over the terrain.

Blade breathed easily, adopting a natural rhythm, determined to stay after the thing until he dropped from exhaustion or caught it. In the back of his mind he wondered if the red-eyed monster might still be about, and he wavered for a few strides before reminding himself he was a Warrior and Warriors never let fear get the better of them.

The pale creature maintained a steady lead, never gaining or losing ground, bearing to the south.

If not for the full moon, Blade would have found the going extremely difficult. He tripped once on a root but righted himself quickly. Every now and then a limb snatched at his vest or gouged him in the cheek.

For several minutes the chase continued. The creature angled to the west, seldom looking back, apparently heading for a specific destination.

Blade lost all track of where he was. He guessed they were passing to the east of the castle. To his annoyance, the thing ran even faster and gained a wider lead. Even Rikki wouldn't be able to overtake it, he realized, but he stubbornly kept running.

The creature paused to look at its pursuer, then forged ahead, darting into a group of saplings and disappearing.

Not again, Blade reflected, sprinting to the stand and barging through the slender trees. Not until he broke from cover and saw the mausoleums did he realize he was at the border of the yard.

There was no sign of the thing.

Damn!

Furious at losing it, Blade walked into the open and looked in all directions. Where had the creature gone? Despite its demonstrated fleetness, the thing couldn't have crossed the yard in the time he took to reach the edge of the woods. Was it hiding behind one of the tombs? Unslinging the rifle, he moved to the nearest mausoleum and circled it.

Nothing.

Blade went to the next, then the next, and nowhere was there a clue to the creature's whereabouts. Mystified, he moved to the middle of the yard and halted. Now he didn't have any proof to show Hickok and Geronimo. All that effort had been wasted.

A sharp gust of wind from the north caused the trees to rustle and brought something with it—the faint sound of music.

Shocked, Blade gazed at the darkened castle. Were his ears playing tricks on him or did he really hear the soft strains of a melodious instrumental wafting through the air? As he strode toward the structure, the volume increased slightly. There could be no doubt. Somewhere in the bowels of the edifice someone was playing music.

He considered fetching his friends and letting them hear for themselves, but what if the music stopped before they came back? Neither of them would believe him. They'd laugh in his face and claim he was going off the deep end, and being humiliated once a night was more than enough for him.

Blade debated whether to investigate further, then thought of his friends slumbering unprotected back at camp. Reluctantly, he retraced his footsteps. At daybreak he would return to the castle and find a way in. Somehow, he intuitively knew the secret to the many mysteries they'd encountered lay within that foreboding monument from ancient times.

He covered half the distance when a guttural snarl off to his left drew him up short. Was it a mutation or a normal predator? His eyes roving over the murky vegetation, he proceeded warily. Between the 45-70 and his Bowies he should be able to handle anything that came along except for dinosaur-sized beasts with glowing red eyes.

Blade reached the camp without mishap and found his buddies still sleeping peacefully. He immediately fed fuel to the fire, and when the flames were high enough he sat back and draped his forearms on his knees. Jenny's beautiful image filled his thoughts, so he spent the next hour reviewing their disagreement over when to bind and another argument they'd had over what to name their first boy. She'd been so proud of him after his Naming, and a discussion about the importance of selecting the perfect name led to a consideration of the ones they'd want to bestow on their own children. Both of them liked Judy or Lisa for a girl, but they clashed where their future male offspring were concerned. Jenny wanted to call their first-born boy Gabriel. Blade wanted a more colorful name, but his wife-to-be absolutely refused to have any son of hers be called Tarzan.

The remaining hours until daylight were uneventful. Blade kept the fire roaring, making two additional trips to gather wood before the first streaks of light tinged the eastern sky. He rose and stretched, grateful the night was over.

Unexpectedly, from the direction of the castle, came a series of three strident, sustained musical notes.

Hickok and Geronimo were on their feet before the sounds faded. The gunman's hands hovered over his Colts as he swung from side to side, not yet fully awake but trying to identify the source of the noise.

"What the blazes was that?"

"Sounded like a bugle or a trumpet," Blade speculated.

"Who'd be playing music at this time of day?" Hickok asked grumpily. "They should have their head examined."

"This day begins as strangely as the last one ended," Geronimo commented.

"I'm glad both of you heard that bugle," Blade said.

"You are?" Geronimo responded.

"Yep. Because now you'll believe me when I tell you I heard music last night when I was standing near the mausoleums."

Geronimo was all interest. "What were you doing there?"

"I chased one of those nymphs."

A protracted groan issued from Hickok. "Terrific," he muttered. "I'm not up five minutes and already we're talking about the phantom fairies."

"Why don't we eat breakfast, then investigate the castle," Blade suggested.

"Do we get to kick in the door if no one answers our knock?" Hickok inquired.

"Yes. I get the feeling someone is playing us for fools, and I want to get to the bottom of this whole business."

"Okay. Then count me in, pard."

Blade picked up his rifle. "I'll go bag us some game."

"There's no need to go hunting on my account," Geronimo said. "I like to eat a light meal in the morning. Jerky and water will do me just fine."

"Same here. I'm not in the mood for stuffed pigeon with all the trimmings," Hickok added.

"Suit yourself."

They sat near the fire and munched on the venison while all around them the woodland came alive with the songs of birds and the rustling of animals.

"Tell me more about the thing you went after?" Hickok prompted.

"There's not much to reveal because I couldn't get a good look at it. All I know is the creature is light colored and runs faster than I do."

"Must be part cheetah," Geronimo quipped.

"Why didn't you shoot the critter?" Hickok asked.

"It didn't make a move to attack. Besides, what if the thing is part human?" Blade replied.

"Then it shouldn't be waltzin' around monster-infested

country in the middle of nowhere,'' Hickok declared. ''Any lamebrain stupid enough to pull such a stunt deserves to have his fool head blown off.''

Geronimo glanced at the buckskin-clad Warrior. ''Need I point out that *we* are waltzing around monster-infected country in the middle of nowhere?''

''It's different with us.''

''How so?''

''We know what we're doing.''

Geronimo turned to Blade. ''Did any of that make sense to you?''

''No.''

''Good. For a second there, I thought it was me.''

''Was that another cut?'' Hickok wanted to know.

After finishing their meal, they doused the fire, donned their backpacks and tramped toward the castle. Geronimo took the lead. On all sides birds greeted the rising of the sun by joining in full chorus.

Breathing in the crisp air, Blade felt invigorated. Gone were the doubts and subtle fears of the night before. He was supremely confident they'd be able to deal with any threat, overcome any obstacle.

Geronimo constantly searched for tracks. When they reached the general area where the red-eyed monstrosity had been, he crouched. ''Hey, take a look at this.''

Butterflies fluttered in Blade's stomach when he laid eyes on more of the gigantic three-toed tracks.

''Now we know what makes those,'' Hickok remarked.

''These seem a bit smaller than the ones we saw yesterday,'' Geronimo mentioned.

''They look the same to me,'' the gunfighter said.

''What's your opinion, Blade?'' Geronimo asked.

The giant pursed his lips thoughtfully. He honestly couldn't decide whether there was a size difference, but he did know he didn't like the idea of two of the brutes being abroad. ''I don't know,'' he said.

"We're lucky none have shown up near the Home," Geronimo stated.

Hickok chuckled. "If we're lucky, maybe some of those wood nymphs will follow us back to the compound. We can set a snare and catch one of the rascals. I'm sure the rest of the Family will be tickled pink to see a genuine wonder in person. Or whatever."

"I can't wait until you see one yourself," Blade said.

"I hope you won't get upset if I don't hold my breath."

Geronimo took the point again, his eyes glued to the soil. "If there were other creatures here last night, they didn't leave a single footprint.

"*If?*" Blade repeated.

"You know what I mean."

"Certainly. You're a graduate of the Hickok school of blathering idiocy."

"Whoa!" Hickok exclaimed. "Now that definitely was a cut."

"Perish forbid."

The gunfighter snickered. "No doubt about it. You've definitely been spendin' too much time with Plato. You're startin' to use the same highfalutin words he does."

"At least he speaks English."

"Wow. Another cut. You're on a roll, pard."

A short while later they were close enough to distinguish the large individual stones composing the battlement. In anxious silence they neared the east side of the castle when they heard a familiar sound.

The buzzing of the miniature plane.

CHAPTER SEVEN

Warily the three youths neared the castle wall, using every available cover. At the edge of the forest, when they hid behind trees and scanned the blue sky, it didn't take long to spot their aerial nemesis.

The small plane was flying in a circle around the castle, just above the turrets, continually performing the same pattern.

"What do you reckon it's doing?" Hickok whispered.

"Looking for us," Geronimo guessed.

Blade regarded the aircraft solemnly. Whoever controlled the plane would employ it to try and stop them from entering. He'd made the mistake of letting the craft dive-bomb them yesterday; he wasn't about to let history repeat itself. "Gernimo, take it down."

"With pleasure," the Blackfoot replied, raising the Winchester to his right shoulder. He patiently aimed, tracking the craft's flight and waiting for the right moment.

"We don't have all day," Hickok said.

"Hold your horses," Geronimo retorted. The plane was

over the southeast turret, its tiny propeller a blur, moving faster than a bird in flight. He inhaled deeply, steadied the barrel and fired.

A shower of sparks and metal exploded from the center of the aircraft, and it went into a steep spiral, tendrils of black and white smoke trailing in its wake. Narrowly missing the rampart, the plane slanted toward the edge of the woods, diving straight at the trio.

Blade awoke to the danger first. Such a small craft posed little threat, but the load it undoubtedly carried did. "Scatter" he shouted, turning and dashing northward. He prayed the others were doing the same. Five yards he covered. Ten. A wide tree trunk on the right offered the sanctuary he needed, and he ducked behind it at the same second the aircraft hit the earth.

The resultant explosion was deafening. Trees buckled or shook. The very ground trembled as if from a quake. Dust and leaves and bits of wood formed a choking cloud vastly larger than the one before.

Hugging the grass, Blade felt the ground move under him. He held his mouth down low to avoid breathing in the swirling cloud and waited for it to disperse. Dirt and jagged pieces of timber rained down, covering him from head to toe. Impatient to learn the fate of his friends, he peered at the spot where the plane struck but saw no movement.

Gradually the cloud dissipated. Blade rose and moved closer to the impact point. "Geronimo! Hickok! Where are you?"

Silence greeted his cry.

Over a dozen trees had been toppled or shattered by the explosion and littered the ground in a jumbled mass. Falling leaves formed a carpet over everything.

"Hickok! Geronimo!" Blade called out again.

"Over here," the Blackfoot responded, appearing from behind an oak situated 20 yards to the south.

"Where's Nathan?"

Geronimo blinked. "I don't know. I thought he was with you."

"I haven't seen him since we took cover."

They walked slowly toward the center of the blast area, scouring the tangled trunks and branches.

"Hickok!" Geronimo yelled. "Answer us!"

Anxiety tugged at Blade's mind. If anything had happened to the colorful gunfighter, he'd never forgive himself. The idea to travel to the castle had been exclusively his; he was directly responsible for the fate of his friends. He shoved a busted section of limb aside and bent down to peer under a fallen tree resting on top of another downed monarch of the forest.

"Hickok! Hickok!" Geronimo kept shouting, turning every which way. "Quit playing games and tell us where you're at."

No answer was forthcoming.

Not until the two of them reached the middle of the flattened vegetation did Geronimo voice the concern uppermost on their minds.

"What if he's dead?"

"We won't stop searching until we find him."

"He must be buried under one of these trees," Geronimo guessed. "Maybe he was flattened like a pancake."

Blade scanned the ground, dreading the very thought. "We don't know that," he said gruffly. "Don't assume the worst."

"He might be a royal pain in the neck sometimes, but deep down he's one of the most decent guys I know," Geronimo lamented. "You couldn't ask for a more loyal friend."

"Will you quit talking like he's dead?" Blade snapped.

Geronimo began moving brush, his features downcast. "I'd never tell him to his face, but I'm proud to know him. To tell the truth, I even liked his sense of humor."

From ten yards to the east, from under a pile of shorn

branches and uprooted vegetation, came a triumphant bellow. "Aha! I heard that!"

"Uh-oh," Geronimo said.

Blade hastened over and got there just as the gunfighter succeeded in shoving the branches off and slowly stood. "Are you okay?"

"Oh, sure," Hickok replied, coughing. "I love being blown to smithereens."

"What happened?"

"I don't want to talk about it," Hickok stated, checking to ensure his prized revolvers were still in their holsters.

Blade brushed several leaves from the lean youth's left shoulder. "You had us worried to death. Why didn't you answer when we were shouting? The least you can do is explain."

Hickok bowed his head as if ashamed. "I tripped," he mumbled.

"You what?"

"Tripped. I was runnin' to beat the band when my foot got caught on this bush and down I went. Then the blamed plane hit, and I felt certain my number was up. The concussion must have knocked me out for a bit, because the next thing I knew I heard voices and there you guys were yakkin' about me."

"You were lucky," Blade said.

"Tell me about it."

Geronimo walked toward them, snickering. "Did I hear correctly, clumsy? You tripped?"

"And did I hear you say that you *like* my sense of humor?" Hickok countered.

"Me? Give me a break. The explosion rattled your brain."

"I heard you," Hickok stated. "Don't try to weasel your way out of this."

The Blackfoot straightened up indignantly. "Indians never weasel."

"Do they lie?"

"Definitely not."

"Then you're not an Indian."

"All right, already," Blade interjected. "We have more important things to concern us than Hickok's sense of humor."

"See?" The gunfighter beamed. "Even you admit I have one."

Sighing, Blade pivoted and started toward the castle. His gaze alighted on the base of the east wall, and surprise halted him in midstride. "Look!" he exclaimed.

The others focused on the building.

Where before there stood a solid wall, there was now a wide crack running from the ground to a height of ten feet. The force of the explosion had wrenched the very foundation, causing the massive stones to shift and split. A yard wide at the bottom, the crack tapered to a few inches at the top. Beyond lay impenetrable darkness.

Stunned by the discovery, the three of them converged on the wall.

"I don't see nothing movin' in there," Hickok commented.

"Are we going in?" Geronimo asked.

"I am," Blade declared. "You two can stay outside if you want."

"What's that crack supposed to mean?" Hickok demanded. "One for all, remember? Where you go, big guy, we go."

"I hate to say this," Geronimo said, "but Nathan is right."

The gunfighter chuckled. "Am I on a roll, or am I on a roll?"

Blade trained the Marlin on the opening and listened for strains of music or other sounds from within, but all he heard was the whisper of the breeze. He stopped at the wall and felt a cool draft on his face. A dank scent tingled his nostrils.

"Looks like the inside of Geronimo's noggin' in there," Hickok noted.

"Want me to make a torch?" the Blackfoot volunteered.

"Go ahead," Blade directed. He tentatively leaned into the crack and distinguished the outlines of a wide corridor but no sign of life. The interior resembled a tomb.

"I imagine whoever owned the flyin' contraption is a bit riled at us right about now," Hickok mentioned. "We'd best be extra careful."

"At least we won't have to worry about them using explosives on us when we're inside," Blade said.

"True, but who knows what other tricks these yahoos have up their sleeves?"

Blade leaned against the wall and waited for Geronimo to construct a makeshift torch.

First the Blackfoot selected a suitable length of straight limb, then chomped off the thin offshoots. Next he went to a pine tree and hacked away a section of bark, exposing the sap-coated trunk. Quickly he rubbed the thick end of the limb back and forth across the sap until it was caked with the sticky substance. Pivoting, he began collecting dried leaves into a pile. Once he had enough, he placed the end of the limb in the middle of the pile and used his left hand to pack the leaves onto the sap. Finally, he started a small fire with his flint, dipped the torch into the flames until it caught, then stamped out the fire.

"Here we go," Geronimo said, rejoining them.

Hickok feigned a yawn. "Is it still the twenty-first century?"

"Very funny."

"Let's go," Blade declared, easing through the crack. He moved a few feet and waited for the others. The moment Geronimo entered, the flickering torchlight illuminated the high corridor for a considerable distance, revealing stone walls and a stone floor.

"Reminds me of a cave," Hickok commented.

"Don't let your guard down for an instant," Blade cautioned, leading the way. He spied a recessed doorway on the right and stealthily headed toward it, bothered by the pervasive silence. There should be noise of some kind. He knew people were living there; he'd seen one of them. So where were they?

A large wooden door materialized in the shadows.

Holding the Marlin in his left hand, Blade reached for the black handle and paused when the latch clicked loudly. Anyone on the other side was bound to have heard. Standing to one side, he pulled the door open.

Within was a musty chamber as inky as the corridor.

Cautiously entering, Blade placed his back to the wall while his friends followed. Revealed by the torch was an enormous living room containing two sofas, a half-dozen chairs, and in one corner, incredibly, a grand piano.

"Wow," Hickok breathed.

"Everything is in perfect condition," Geronimo said.

Blade had noticed the same thing. He realized there must be countless treasures from the past on every floor. Walking through the castle was like taking a stroll back in time to the days before the war. "Stay close," he instructed them, as he moved out to the corridor. Taking a right, he proceeded deeper into the fascinating enigma.

For a good 20 yards there were only blank walls, then a stairway appeared on the left.

Stepping closer to investigate, Blade found there were steps leading upward and a flight going down. From below wafted a musty, moist smell.

"Which way, pard?" Hickok asked.

Before Blade could answer, they all heard a rustling noise and glanced up at the next landing. Standing in the open, her long, dark hair partially concealing her features, was the woman in the white dress. As soon as they laid eyes on her, she bolted.

"After her!" Blade cried, bounding up the stairs three at a stride and outpacing his companions before he took the first turn. Ahead was the mystery woman, fleeing as if her life depended on it, the lower half of her dress billowing behind her, already at the next landing. He saw her dart down a corridor and increased his speed.

"Wait for us," Hickok shouted.

But Blade had no intention of letting the woman escape. He attained the landing and spied her racing figure far ahead, her white dress making her easy to spot. "Wait!" he cried. "We won't hurt you."

Apparently she didn't believe him because she kept on running.

Blade took off, disregarding the fact that darkness now enveloped him. He thought he saw the woman dart to the left, possibly through a doorway, and he concentrated on the exact spot as he narrowed the gap. Sure enough, he found an open door and rushed recklessly inside, then halted. Not a trace of light broke the solid curtain of black, and he couldn't determine where the walls were or if there was furniture scattered about. Since he couldn't see her but suspected she was hiding nearby, he decided to try coaxing her out. "I know you're in here, lady," he declared in his most mature tone. "You have nothing to be afraid of. My friends and I have come in peace."

The black curtain mocked him with its silence.

"Please believe me," Blade urged. "We only want to talk to you, nothing more. Come out where I can see you."

That was when the net dropped over his shoulders.

CHAPTER EIGHT

Blade instinctively elevated his arms to ward off the clinging mesh, but he was too late to prevent the loops of rope from draping over his torso and falling almost to the floor. He took a step backwards, or tried to, and regretted his stupidity when his lower legs became entangled and he lost his balance. Down he went, toppling halfway through the doorway, his right shoulder bearing the brunt of the impact and making him wince as the stone floor jarred him to the bone. Rolling onto his stomach, he attempted to push erect, but the clinging net restricted his arms to the point where he couldn't move more than an inch.

Light thuds sounded to his rear.

Mystified, Blade tried to roll over again. Strong hands gripped his ankles and started to pull him into the room. Realizing he was helpless and anticipating he might be shot or stabbed at any second, he tilted his neck and yelled at the top of his lungs. "Hickok! Geronimo! They've got me!"

A hard object, perhaps a fist, rammed into the fledgling Warrior's back.

Blade arched his back, grit his teeth against the pain and renewed his struggle to turn over. He let go of the Marlin, which was flush with his body, and tried to force his huge arms outward, exerting all of his prodigious strength. More blows rained down, but he ignored them. The fact his assailants weren't using knives or clubs made him think they wanted to capture him alive, which was little consolation under the circumstances. He strained as he'd never strained before, every muscle bulging, and slowly, inch by inch, the net began to loosen.

A loud scraping sound suddenly punctuated the pounding of the fists.

Engrossed in breaking free at all costs, Blade thought nothing of the noise until a heavy object that felt like solid iron crashed down onto his head and shoulders. His consciousness swirled, and for a second he was on the verge of blacking out. He vaguely registered the drumming of footsteps, and then bright light engulfed him and familiar voices brought overwhelming relief.

"Here he is, Geronimo!"

"He's caught in a net!"

"What was your first clue?"

"Get him out, quick."

"You get him out. I can cover better than you can."

As the net was pulled off, Blade twisted his head and blinked up at his friends. Hickok stood with his Colts leveled, glaring into the chamber, while Geronimo was tugging on the net with one hand and holding the torch aloft with the other. "Took you long enough," Blade muttered, his shoulders and back throbbing, and then thought of his attackers. "Where are they?"

"Who?" Hickok responded.

"The ones who jumped me," Blade stated, sitting up.

"We didn't see anyone," Geronimo said.

"Impossible," Blade declared. "I think there were two of them, and they didn't go out this door." He clasped the Marlin and stood up. Nearby lay an overturned wooden chair. He realized one of his foes had used it to strike him and wished he could return the favor. Incredibly, there was no one else in the chamber.

But there were books, thousands and thousands of them, filling bookcases that lined all four walls from the floor to the ceiling. In the middle of the room was a large mahogany table and five chairs, brothers to the one lying near the doorway.

"It's a library," Blade said, stepping over to the table. His eyes made a complete circuit of the room, seeking an exit. There was none. He did discover how they'd managed to drop the net on him. The bookcases on either side of the door weren't completely filled, which led him to conclude his attackers had climbed up and perched there with the net taut between them until he came in. If so, it meant the woman in white deliberately led him into an ambush.

"Did you happen to get a look at the ones who jumped you?" Geronimo inquired.

"Nope," Blade replied. "It was too dark."

"How did the vermin escape without us spotting them?" Hickok asked.

Blade recalled a book he'd read several years ago entitled *The Complete Sherlock Holmes*. "There has to be a secret passage in here. Spread out and try to find it."

They each took a portion of wall and conducted a hasty search, moving books aside and thumping on the back panels in an effort to locate a concealed door. After several minutes each of them stopped and stared at the others.

"This is hopeless," Geronimo said. "There are too many shelves, too many books. It could take us a year."

"Then we'll keep going from room to room until we flush them out again," Blade proposed.

"What makes you think we will?" the gunfighter asked.

"They obviously don't want us in the castle. Why else did they pounce on me?"

Hickok shrugged. "They probably mistook you for that monster with the red eyes."

"Can't you be serious for one minute?"

"Okay. Maybe they figured you were one of the wood nymphs."

"You're hopeless."

"Yeah, but I've got style."

Blade walked into the corridor and glanced in both directions. There were more doors on this floor, including some he'd passed as he pursued the woman, and he nodded at the closest one. "Let's check it out."

"We're right behind you," Hickok said, replacing the Colts. "Just try not to get lost this time."

"Not funny," Blade said, leading the way.

The gunfighter leaned toward Geronimo and snickered. "Boy, a few bumps and bruises and he goes all to pieces."

Blade looked over his shoulder. "I heard that."

"Good ears. You must be part bunny rabbit."

Sighing, the giant opened the next door and peered in at a plush sitting room complete with thick carpeting, a half-dozen easy chairs, and a gold-gilded sofa fit for a palace.

Hickok whistled in appreciation. "Too bad we can't lug any of this stuff back with us. That sofa would look great in my cabin."

"You don't have a cabin yet," Geronimo noted. "Only married couples are alloted cabins."

"I'll be married some day."

"My condolences to your future bride."

"Clam up, you two," Blade snapped. He went to the next room, and the next, and in each found the same extravagant furnishings, the same immaculate conditions, the same evidence of greath wealth. The thought brought him up short.

Wait a minute!

Immaculate conditions?

Blade stared at the floor, then the walls. He ran his fingers over the stone and examined the tips. "Have you guys noticed something?" he asked.

"Do you mean other than you actin' weird?" Hickok rejoined.

"There isn't any dust," Blade informed them.

"Dust?" the gunfighter repeated.

"Yeah, you know. As in dirt and grime and all that. These walls and the floor are clean enough to eat off of, which means someone mops and dusts on a regular basis."

"You're right, pard," Hickok said, glancing around. "We must be up against a bunch of irate house cleaners. Or is that castle cleaners?"

Geronimo offered his rifle to Blade. "You're welcome to shoot him with my gun if you want."

"Why waste the bullet?" Blade said and resumed hunting for clues. They covered every room on the second floor, then went up to the third. Again they found chambers filled with furniture, ornaments and paintings that would have cost a small fortune prior to the Big Blast. But evidence someone lived there eluded them.

"How many floors are there in this place?" Hickok asked as they made toward the last doorway along the corridor.

"There must be six or seven in a building this size," Blade guessed.

"We can be here all day."

"If you have a better idea on how we can discover who's behind all of this, I'm open to suggestions."

"I was just thinkin' about Attila."

"What about him?"

"We're supposed to be on guard duty tomorrow night. If we don't show up, he'll be as mad as a wet cat."

Geronimo snorted. "You have such a wonderful way with words, Nathan."

"We'll be back at the Home by the time our shift

starts,'' Blade predicted. ''Even if we stay over here tonight, we'll have all day tomorrow to make the return trip.''

''Are you plannin' to stay over?''

''It depends on how things turn out.''

Hickok chuckled. ''You can't fool me. The real reason you want to stay another night is you're hopin' to see those fairies again.''

''Please use my gun,'' Geronimo begged.

Blade turned to the door and reached for the knob when from somewhere far below, seeming to come from the very bowels of the earth, came a faint scream, a terrified shriek that lasted for a good 30 seconds and abruptly ended in awful silence. ''Let's go,'' he barked and made a move toward the stairs.

''We can't,'' Geronimo stated.

''Why not?''

''The torch is going out.''

Sure enough, the flames were much lower and might extinguish completely within the next couple of minutes. ''There must be something we can use to make another one,'' Blade said, then he opened the door.

A music room unfolded before their wondering eyes, with a harp in one corner, a bass on a stand in another, a violin mounted in a case on the south wall, and another piano, this one smaller than its counterpart downstairs. the only furniture consisted of two chairs, a small sofa and a narrow cabinet against the rear wall.

''There doesn't appear to be anything we can use,'' Geronimo said.

Blade was about to close the door when his gaze fell on the polished piano. An idea occurred to him, and he hastened to the maple cabinet.

''What are you doing?'' Hickok asked.

''Looking for whatever they used to polish the furniture and the piano.''

''What in the world for?''

"It just might be flammable," Blade responded, opening the panel doors. There were four narrow shelves crammed with odds and ends—several bows for the violin, music books, a harmonica, three glass bottles partially filled with liquid substances, folded pieces of cloth and more. He raised one of the bottles and read its label: EVERLASTING WOOD POLISH. Unscrewing the cap, he raised the bottle to his nose and promptly regretted doing so. An acrid scent capable of gagging a horse made him turn aside and cough. On closer inspection of the label he found two words printed at the bottom: WARNING. FLAMMABLE.

"Bingo," he announced.

Geronimo had walked to the sofa and was examining the stitching in the smooth, pink fabric covering the upholstered seat and back. "Your knives can cut this easier than my tomahawks," he remarked.

Blade went over and handed the bottle to the Blackfoot, then crouched. Drawing his left Bowie, he proceeded to cut six-inch wide strips of pink fabric, each about a foot long, and draped them over the armrest. After accumulating four such strips, he slid the knife into the sheath and stood.

Hickok was standing guard at the door.

"The owners won't be very pleased at having their furniture destroyed," Geronimo mentioned.

"And I'm not overjoyed at having someone beat on me with a chair," Blade replied. "Which makes us even." He took one of the strips and poured the polish over it until the fabric was soaked, then did the same with the remaining three.

Meanwhile, the torch had sputtered down to a few lingering fingers of flame.

"Hold it out," Blade directed, clasping the drenched strips in both hands. He had to work quickly or suffer burnt fingers. Extending his arms to the side, he waited until the torch was almost out and he could barely see the limb, then he whipped the strips around and wrapped them tightly about the smoldering end. No sooner had he secured them and drew his hands back than the torch flared to life again with a sizzling sound and a puff of smoke.

"Pretty clever, pard," Hickok complimented him.

"Now let's go see where the scream came from," Blade proposed and hastened from the music room to the stairs, his companions right beside him. They paused at the landing to listen.

"Think it was the woman in the white dress?" Hickok wondered.

"No telling," Blade said, moving slowly downward. "But from now on we stick together no matter what."

"Shucks. Do you mean I can't go chasin' after any wood nymphs?"

"Will you stop already with the wood nymphs?"

"Sure. Just tryin' to cheer you up after the lickin' you took."

"Do me a favor."

"Anything."

"Try and cheer Geronimo up for a change."

"Hey, don't involve me," the Blackfoot said softly. "He's your problem."

"Who are you callin' a problem?" Hickok demanded.

"Quiet," Blade said sternly.

The gunfighter, of course, had to get in the last word. "Boy, what a couple of grumps."

In silence they descended to the ground floor and halted. Blade stood at the edge of the next flight of steps and peered into the inky domain below. The air felt cooler, and the dank scent was stronger. He gripped the Marlin and went down cautiously, carefully placing one foot after the other. Another stone corridor, narrower than those upstairs, appeared below, with branches running in four different directions. At the next landing they stopped to survey the lower level.

To Blade's amazement, they'd discovered a subterranean network of passageways and rooms. A half-dozen doors were visible along each branch. Even more surprising was the fact that the stairs continued down to yet another level. He speculated on how far down the levels actually went. If there were as many floors below ground as above, then trying to search every square inch of the castle was an impossible task.

The dank, cool air intensified, and a slight breeze caressed their faces.

"This place gives me the creeps," Geronimo said.

"How can there be a breeze down here?" Hickok asked.

"I don't know," Blade admitted, wrestling with the decision of whether to go lower or check this level first. He believed the scream came from farther down, but the idea of venturing into the castle's nether realms intimidated him. His vivid imagination created all sorts of horrid beasts waiting below for the chance to pounce on them. Before he could make up his mind, however, an unforeseen event occurred.

Hickok cleared his throat. "Excuse me," he said ever so politely.

"What is it?" Blade responded, turning to find the gunfighter staring up the stairs.

"We've got company."

Startled, Blade turned and couldn't believe his eyes when he saw the lady in white standing not ten feet away.

CHAPTER NINE

This time the woman didn't flee. She stood calmly in the middle of a step and regarded them with transparent curiosity. Her eyes were a striking green, her lips a rosy red, both contrasting sharply with her exceptionally pale complexion.

None of the three youths spoke. They were collectively mesmerized by her lovely presence, and not even the gunfighter thought to level a weapon at her.

After studying them for a moment, the woman smiled, exposing even rows of pearly teeth, and addressed them in a soft, oddly seductive voice reminiscent of a gentle breeze on a romantic, moonlight night. "Why, you're mere boys."

Hickok roused himself from the spell first, taking a menacing stride and wagging a Colt at her. "Who are you callin' boys, lady? I'll have you know two of us are Warriors."

The woman's composure was unruffled. "What, pray tell, is a Warrior?"

Nipping Hickok's response in the bud, Blade stepped

forward. "We'll ask the questions here, if you don't mind. Who are you? What is this place? Why were we attacked?"

"Such an inquisitive nature in so handsome a youngster," the woman responded.

"You're evading the question," Blade told her harshly.

"Aren't you being a bit presumptuous, young man?" she countered. "The three of you are the intruders, not me. You broke into our home, violated our sanctuary. If anyone should answer questions, it's you."

Blade didn't know what to do. Technically, she was right, and as someone who'd been trained since childhood to respect both his elders and the property of others, he felt acute guilt over his actions. Thankfully, Geronimo came to his rescue.

"We didn't break in, lady. We walked in after the plane you sent to bomb us crashed and opened a crack in the castle wall."

The woman stared at the Blackfoot for a few moments, her features inscrutable, then nodded. "Very well. Perhaps we both have some explaining to do." She gestured distastefully at the subterranean level. "But there's no need to question each other on these stairs. Why not come with me to the sitting room where we can converse like civilized adults?"

Blade wondered if her comment was a subtle slur. He decided to let it pass for the time being and nodded. "All right. We'll follow you. But don't try any tricks or you'll regret it."

Her eyes narrowed accustingly. "Is it customary where you're from to threaten an unarmed woman?"

"No," Blade promptly answered. "And it's not customary to throw a net over someone else and beat them to a pulp."

She viewed him from head to toe with an amused expression. "Funny. You don't look like pulp to me."

Motioning for his friends to stay close, Blade started to ascend the steps but managed only two strides when a strange thing happened. The woman recoiled as if in great fear and placed her forearms over her eyes.

"Stay back!" she blurted.

Bewildered, Blade halted. "What's the matter?"

"It's your torch," the woman disclosed. "The light hurts my eyes. Please don't get too close."

"Why does the light hurt?" Blade asked suspiciously.

She rotated so her back was to them and responded over her left shoulder. "Becuase I've spent my entire life in this castle, and the only time I venture outdoors is at night. Any bright light is terribly painful to me."

"We don't want to hurt you," Blade assured her. "You lead the way, and we'll stay far enough back to keep the light from bothering your eyes."

"Thank you," the woman said, climbing the stairs slowly.

Exchanging puzzled glances, the three of them trailed the woman to the ground floor. She led them down the corridor to an open door and paused at the jamb.

"Is it necessary for you to bring the torch into the room?"

"We can't see in the dark, lady," Hickok declared.

"You can't?" she responded, a hint of sarcasm in her tone. "In that case, I'll light several candles. Would that satisfy you?"

"Yes," Blade said. "We'll wait until the candles are lit before we extinguish our torch."

"Don't you trust me?"

"No."

She peeked at him and grinned. "Brutal honesty. I like that trait in a man."

Blade made no response. He watched her go into the room and looked at his friends. "What do you think?"

"I think we can trust her about as far as we can toss

this castle,'' Hickok said.

''This must be a ploy of some kind,'' Geronimo stated. ''Why didn't she talk to us earlier when she had the chance? Why did she wait until we were about to investigate the underground levels? And what connection does she have to the scream we heard?''

''She has a lot to answer for,'' Blade conceded. ''We'll play along with her game for the time being, but stay sharp. Let me do most of the talking.''

''Why you?'' Hickok inquired.

''What difference does it make?'' Blade rejoined.

''Let Blade do it,'' Geronimo interjected. ''He'll ask intelligent questions.''

''And I wouldn't?'' Hickok retorted.

A subdued glow filled the room. ''You can come in now,'' announced the woman in white.

''Put out the torch,'' Blade said.

Geronimo lowered the burning end to the floor and moved it back and forth across the stones, gradually snuffing the flames. For added measure he tramped on the torch until smoldering red embers remained. ''That should do it.''

His rifle leveled, Blade walked into the chamber and halted. Seated on a sofa against the opposite wall was the woman. A fireplace stood to her right. Several chairs were positioned at various points, and he moved to one and sat down.

Geronimo took another chair, but Hickok remained standing near the door, his thumbs hooked in his gunbelt.

''You can sit down, too, young man,'' the woman addressed the gunfighter.

''I'll stand, lady, if you don't mind,'' Hickok replied. ''And even if you do.''

''There's no need to be rude.''

''My apologies, ma'am,'' Hickok said, his mouth creasing in a grin that belied his statement.

The woman focused on the giant. "I trust you have better manners than your friend?"

"You'll have to excuse Hickok," Blade said. "He tends to get upset when someone tries to kill him."

"I haven't tried to kill him."

"We'll have to take your word for that," Blade said, staring at the two large candles on the mantle. How had she lit them so fast? Did she own matches? The Family still possessed a substantial portion of the dozens of cases Carpenter had stocked, although they were strictly rationed. Flints were the preferred means of starting fires, and by the time every boy and girl in the Family turned eight they were proficient at doing so.

"Why don't we start over again and try to get off on the right foot?" the woman asked. "My name is Endora, mistress of Castle Orm."

Blade had never known anyone called Endora before. "What an unusual name," he commented.

The lady misconstrued. "My great-grandfather named the castle after a legendary beastie believed to inhabit remote lakes in Scotland. He saw one of the monsters once, before coming to America, and read a book on them by a man named Holiday. Took the sighting as a sort of omen, he did."

"Your great-grandfather was Scottish?"

"Aye, he was. And stout Scottish blood flows in our veins still."

"My name is Blade." The Warrior introduced himself and pointed at his buddies. "Geronimo is the one with the tomahawks, and the rude one is called Hickok."

"I seem to recall reading those names somewhere," Endora said thoughtfully, then shook her head. "But no matter. Why have the three of you invaded our castle?"

"We didn't invade it," the gunfighter said. "We walked in through the crack in the wall. How many times do we have to tell you?"

For a moment Endora glared at Hickok. She recovered her composure quickly, though, and smiled at Blade. "Even allowing for the crack, is that any reason to walk into someone else's home without a by-your-leave?"

Blade pursed his lips. There she went again, playing on his guilt. He refused to let her tactic work. "After all the things that happened to us since we arrived, yes, we were justified in entering. We tried knocking, but no one answered the front door."

"Did you ever stop to think there might be a reason? Perhaps we don't like to be disturbed. Perhaps we want to be left to our own devices."

"Who is this 'we' you keep referring to?"

"I don't live here alone," Endora said.

"I know," Blade stated, rubbing a sore spot on his head.

Endora noticed the motion and appreciated its significance. "I'm sorry you were hurt. I truly am. But they thought you were trying to harm me."

"They?"

"My husband and my brother."

"Where are they now?"

"They had business to attend to. They'll be here shortly."

Blade glanced at Hickok, who nonchalantly strolled closer to the door and positioned himself so he'd spot anyone approaching. "Didn't you hear me call out to you? I promised not to harm you."

"How could we know whether you were speaking the truth?" Endora said. "You might have been trying to trick me."

The argument was valid, Blade had to admit. He studied her, trying to guess how old she was and to appraise her character. Her answers were honest enough, but he suspected she was hiding something. There was a trace of—panic?—in her eyes, detectable when he asked questions about the others living in the castle. Why? What did she have to be afraid of? Or was she hiding something?

"Granted," he said. "So I won't hold the beating I took against your husband and brother—for now."

"How gracious of you."

Blade decided to slip in a query she wouldn't be expecting. "By the way, do you happen to know who was screaming a while ago?"

The woman tensed, her hands clenched in her lap, and grinned. "Oh, that was me."

"You?"

"Yes. I bumped into my brother and mistook him for one of you. The shock made me scream my fool head off."

Blade didn't believe her for a second. "That was quite a scream."

She shrugged. "You know how it is when you're scared to death."

"No," Blade said, "I've never been that scared." No sooner did he finish speaking than an image of the red-eyed monster loomed in his mind, and he shook his head to dispel it.

"Then you must be very brave."

"We all are, lady," Hickok chimed in. "That's why you'd best not mess with us or you'll be eatin' lead."

Endora appeared shocked. "You'd threaten a woman?"

The gunfighter smirked. "Makes no nevermind to me who's tryin' to kill me. Anyone who does is history."

"Are there many like him where you come from?" Endora asked Blade.

"No. He's unique."

"Where do you come from, if you don't mind my asking?"

"Faraway," Blade lied. "In a small town northwest of here."

"Which town?"

"I'd rather not say at the moment."

"I see," Endora said, her countenance hardening.

"And why should I politely answer your questions if you're not going to answer any of mine?"

"You have a point," Blade said and gave the first name that popped into his head. "We're from Humboldt."

"How many people live there?"

What would be a reasonable number? Blade asked himself and made a guess. "About two hundred."

"Really? My husband will be interested in hearing that."

"Tell me something," Blade prompted. "I take it your great-grandfather built this place. Why? It's not every day you see a castle in the middle of the Minnesota countryside."

For the first time since they met, Endora laughed, her face relaxing and her hands unfolding in her lap. "Great-grandfather Moray was a wee bit of an eccentric. Before he came to America, he lived by himself on the moors in Scotland. He'd spend every waking minute hiking over those barren wastelands, and he developed quite a passion for them. Thought of the moors as his own private preserve. One day the government went and put a new highway right through the middle of his precious tract of nothing, and it sent him into a rage. He tried to stop them in court. When that failed, he vowed to leave Scotland and never set foot on her soil again." She paused. "Moray came to America and drifted west. Eventually he found this isolated spot and decided to build his new home here. He had all his funds transferred to an American bank and oversaw the construction of the castle. After that he settled down to the life of a country gentleman.

"I take it he survived the war?"

"Yes. The castle is built strong. He also foresaw the war coming and had the underground levels built to live in until the danger of radiation poisoning passed. Our family has lived here ever since."

"And you've had no contact with the outside world?"

"None."

"Why is that?"

The answer came from a totally unexpected source, courtesy of a gruff voice near the right-hand wall. "Because we don't *like* outsiders, boy. That's why."

Taken unawares, Blade swiveled in his chair and discovered two men standing 15 feet away, one with a double-barreled shotgun trained on his chest.

CHAPTER TEN

The newcomers were a bizarre, desperate pair.

Holding the shotgun was the shorter man, a lean, frail figure who was a mere five feet tall. An immaculate, neatly pressed, baggy black suit hung from his frame like the oversized garments on a scarecrow. His head, in proportion to his body, was extremely large, a pumpkin on a broomstick as it were. A cruel slit of a mouth curled downward as he regarded the youths. High cheekbones and a slanting nose gave him an imperious aspect, complimented by his flashing green eyes and bushy brows, and a wild shock of black hair streaked with white crowned his cranium.

Only in one respect did the second man resemble the first. His brows were bushy, even more so, inch-wide strips of thick hairs that would have done justice to a gorilla. And in many respects he was like a huge ape. Seven feet tall, his broad, hunched shoulders gave him a perpetually stooped aspect. His brawny hands, possessing knuckles the size of walnuts, dangled next to his knees. Ill-fitting clothes scarcely contained his enormous arms and barrel chest, and his size 18 feet were naked. Dull brown eyes regarded the trio more in curiosity than in malice.

Blade saw the shotgun wielder pivot toward the doorway.

"Don't even think of it," the man snapped.

Shifting, Blade saw Hickok poised to draw.

"Drop the shotgun, mister," the gunfighter warned.

"No one dictates to Morlock in his own house," the shorter man snapped. "And if you go for those revolvers, I'll blow you in half."

Hickok smiled. "I've got news for you, chump. I'll put a bullet in your brain before you can squeeze the trigger."

"No one is that fast," the man scoffed.

"*I* am," Hickok stated.

Blade was going to admonish the gunfighter to wait when someone else intervened.

"Husband, no!" Endora cried, rising. "There's no need for killing. They've convinced me they have peaceful intentions."

The man called Morlock glanced disdainfully at her. "And you believe them, my dear?"

"Yes, I do. Look at them. They're just boys. They came here from Humboldt, where there are other survivors," Endora said. "And what about their families?"

A weird reaction occurred, and Blade didn't know what to make of it. Morlock perceptibly stiffened at the mention of other survivors, then slowly lowered the shotgun.

"Very well. We must do the proper thing, eh?"

"Please forgive my husband," Endora said, stepping to the man's side. Her shoulders were eight inches higher than his, and the contrast of her stately beauty to his malevolent mien was glaring. "Dearest, I'd like you to meet our guests. This is Blade, Geronimo and Hickok," she said, indicating each in turn.

"Guests, is it? More like intruders to my way of thinking,'' the husband snapped. He handed the shotgun to the apish man, who took it as if grasping an egg.

''We're sorry if we've upset you,'' Blade offered.

''Upset us, hell. You've put us to a lot of trouble, young man, and all because you don't know how to respect the rights of others,'' Morlock said. ''This castle is our home. Don't they teach you any meaning of that word where you come from?''

''Of course they do,'' Blade said defensively.

''Then you'll be so good as to vacate these premises right now.''

Endora cleared her throat. ''Why don't we give them a spot of tea before they leave?''

''Why don't we ask them to move in?'' Morlock responded sarcastically.

Blade had tolerated all the abuse he was willing to stand. He rose, being careful to point the rifle at the floor, and faced the spiteful owner. ''Look, mister, we'll leave just as soon as we get answers to some important questions. For one thing, we'd like to know why you tried to kill us?''

Morlock sneered. ''Don't be absurd. I never tried to kill you, boy.''

''Someone did. First they used a toy plane carrying miniature bombs. And earlier, upstairs, I was attacked and beaten by two men. Tell me it wasn't you.''

''I attacked you upstairs,'' Morlock said. ''I freely admit as much. You and your friends broke into our home. Naturally, I took it as a hostile gesture and took appropriate measures.''

''And the plane?''

''Was obtained by the man who built this castle long ago. He installed a surveillance camera in the nose and rigged the craft to carry miniature bombs, strictly for security purposes. The plane was programmed to spot interlopers and take appropriate action. Don't blame me if it came after you.''

"Do you expect us to swallow that load of manure?" Hickok interjected.

"I don't care what you swallow, young man," Morlock said. "Just so you do it elsewhere."

"Husband, enough," Endora said.

"Enough!" The lord of the manor glanced at his brutish shadow. "Elphinstone, escort them outside. See to it that they depart immediately."

Nodding once, Elphinstone moved forward ponderously, his arms swinging at his sides, the shotgun clutched as if it was a club and not a gun.

"Put the shotgun down," Morlock commanded.

Obediently, like a puppy obeying its master, Elphinstone deposited the weapon.

Blade saw no reason to stay. Trying to interrogate Morlock would be an exercise in futility. "We must relight our torch first," he stated. "Then we'll go."

After a few seconds of deliberation, Morlock agreed. "Very well. But vacate these premises quickly or I won't be held responsible for the consequences."

"Are you threatenin' us?" Hickok asked.

"Take it any way you want, boy," Morlock said.

Motioning at Geronimo, Blade waited until the Blackfoot had touched the torch to a candle and reignited the strips before he walked from the room without a backward glance, his friends right behind him.

"I don't like runnin' with my tail between my legs," Hickok groused.

"We're not running," Blade said. "We're being diplomatic."

"Isn't that the same thing?"

They moved along the corridor toward the cracked wall, their apish escort dogging their heels.

Geronimo looked over his shoulder. "Elphinstone, is that your name? How do you like living here?"

The brute made no reply.

"Wonderful conversationalist," Geronimo quipped.

"Reminds me of you, Nathan."

Blade was pondering the implications of everything they'd learned so far, and he barely noticed when they drew abreast of the stairs. A wavering wail from below broke his concentration and brought him up short. "What was that?"

"Sounded like a woman," Hickok said.

"Let's go see," Geronimo proposed.

Suddenly Elphinstone moved, displaying surprising speed in one so massive, and blocked their access to the steps. He pointed toward the end of the corridor and uttered a raspy order. "Go."

Hickok bristled. "Who do you think you are tellin' us what to do, you overgrown sack of—"

"Enough," Blade stated, grabbing the gunfighter's left arm. "Whatever is down there is none of our business."

"Says you," Hickok responded. "I vote we go check."

"Not now," Blade said, pulling the gunfighter after him down the hall. He let go when Hickok quit resisting.

"Okay, pard, you made your point. But when we get back to the Home, I'm not tellin' a soul about this escapade of ours."

"Why not?" Geronimo inquired.

"Because I don't want anyone to learn I hang around with a pair of wimps."

"We'll talk outside," Blade stated and hastened his pace, grateful for the slash of bright light serving as their beacon out of there. They needed time to collect their thoughts and formulate a plan of action. Whether Hickok realized it or not, Morlock enjoyed a grave advantage, a fact he intended to explain shortly.

Seldom had a sunlit day radiated such beauty as the warm, tranquil setting into which they stepped after reaching the crack.

Blade squinted up at the blue sky, surveyed the lush green trees before them, spotted several sparrows flitting about in the undergrowth, and inhaled deeply.

"Thanks for seeing us out," Geronimo said to Elphinstone, who abruptly wheeled and stalked off. "Next time try not to bend our ears so much."

"Pitiful. Just pitiful," Hickok mumbled, marching into the forest, his posture consistent with his anger.

"Wait for us," Blade said.

"Why should I? I'm embarrassed to know you."

Geronimo still carried the flaming torch. He dropped it on the grass and stamped over and over on the lit end until it was out.

Hickok was still walking away.

"Come on," Blade said, jogging to overtake the cantankerous gunfighter. "I asked you to wait," he said when he caught up.

"No, you didn't. You *told* me to wait. This whole trip you've been actin' like you're top dog and Geronimo and me are common curs. I'm tired of it."

"I didn't mean to offend you."

"I know. But unless Attila appoints you as head of a Warrior Triad, or if some day—heh, heh—you become top Warrior, you've got no right to be bossing us around."

"I'm sorry," Blade said. "Now will you stop and listen?"

"Yeah," Geronimo added. "Try using your head for a change of pace instead of your heart."

Sighing, Hickok halted and swung toward them. "All right. Let me hear what you have to say. But it had better be good or I'm headin' on back to the Home, and nothin' you can say or do will stop me."

Blade nodded. "Fair enough. Try this on for size." He paused and glanced at the castle. "We're not leaving here until we discover the truth. I don't care what that pompous ass in there told us to do."

"Now you're talkin' my language," Hickok said, grinning. "But why'd you let him push us around?"

"Think for a minute. He wasn't about to reveal a thing, and we would have wasted our time trying to pry answers out of him. If we stayed we might have provoked him into using his shotgun and—"

"I could've taken him," Hickok interrupted.

"I know, but you're missing the point. We would have been in the wrong killing him without justification. Remember the course we took on the moral and ethical aspect of killing? A Warrior must never resort to violence unless there is no other alternative. We weren't in imminent danger. Sure, we suspect Morlock lied through his teeth and deliberately set the plane after us, but we can't prove it. And since we did enter their castle without permission, morally and ethically we were in the wrong."

"Only you could turn killin' a cow chip into a philosophy lesson."

"Do you see my point or not?"

"Yep," Hickok admitted begrudgingly. "You're right. But I don't like it none." He scratched his chin and cocked his head. "Even if we didn't have an excuse to blow Morlock away, we had every right to go into those lower levels and find out what was down there. It sounded like someone was sufferin' bad."

"It did," Blade agreed. "But if we'd tried to barge on down there, we would have played into Morlock's hand."

"How do you figure? That jumbo monkey couldn't have stopped us."

"Maybe. But Morlock certainly could have."

"Morlock?"

"Yeah, dummy. Think again. How did Morlock and Elphinstone get into the room where we were talking with Endora?"

"Beats me. I know they didn't come in the door because I was right there."

"Exactly. The only way they could have entered was through a secret passage. I was right. The castle must be honeycombed with hidden corridors enabling them to go anywhere and spy on anyone. And do you think for a minute that Morlock wasn't watching us leave? The moment we tore into Elphinstone, Morlock would have blasted us."

"Hmmmmm. I never thought of that."

"A warrior must keep sharp at all times, Nathan."

"Don't start with another lesson," Hickok stated defensively. "So I made a little mistake. No harm done."

"There could have been," Blade said.

"Okay. What's the plan?"

"We'll stay over another night."

"That's it?"

"Morlock will undoubtedly spy on us. When he learns we're not leaving, he might make a move against us."

"Then we nail the sucker?"

"Then we nail him, if need be."

Geronimo craned his neck to gaze at the battlement. "You know, I feel sorry for the woman. Can you imagine what it must be like for her to be married to Morlock?"

"There's another mystery," Blade said. "How old would you guess Endora to be?"

"I don't know. Twenty-five, maybe," Geronimo answered.

"Me, too. And how old do you think Morlock is?"

"Fifty. Fifty-five."

"Or older. Doesn't it strike you as strange that she would marry someone so much older?"

"Not really. Couples at the Home sometimes have a five or ten year age difference between husband and wife," Geronimo said.

"Yeah, but a thirty year difference?"

Geronimo shrugged. "Maybe there wasn't anyone else she could marry. They said they haven't had any contact with the outside world."

Blade nodded again. "Do you realize what that means?"

Sudden insight caused Geronimo to gape in astonishment. "Wow. I never thought of that."

"Thought of what?" Hickok asked.

"There can only be one explanation," Blade went on.

"Realize what?" Hickok inquired impatiently, looking from one to the other.

"This puts their relationship in a whole new perspective," Geronimo said.

"What the blazes are you two talkin' about?" Hickok snapped. "Would one of you kindly explain it to me?"

"Later," Blade said, staring off in the direction of their camp. "Let's go eat lunch and make our plans for tonight. I want to have everything ready before dark."

Geronimo and Hickok followed, the gunfighter nudging the Blackfoot.

"Would you mind explaining what in the world is going on?"

"We're going to eat lunch."

"That's not what I meant, and you know it."

Geronimo chuckled. "Sorry. There might be a skeleton in their closet."

"Did they bump somebody off?"

"Not that kind of skeleton."

"Then what kind?"

"The family tree kind."

Hickok hissed in frustration. "Skeletons. Trees. I'm beginning to think you've lost your marbles, pard."

"At least I had some to start with."

CHAPTER ELEVEN

The three of them were in position by nightfall.

Blade sat in the fork of an oak tree 30 feet from their camp and stared at the fire. Eventually one of them must creep out and add fuel to the flames, but for now, thanks to the strategic placement of their backpacks at the south end of the lean-to, the camp gave every impression of being occupied. It had been his idea to stack the backpacks at the one end to block the view of anyone, or anything, approaching from that direction. If he was correct in his hunch, if the creatures followed the same path tonight as last night, then his trap might work.

He glanced down at the ground 12 feet below and shifted to alleviate a cramp in his lower back. All day he'd been bothered by pain from his shoulders to his hips due to the beating he'd sustained. He guessed that Elphinstone had done the pounding. Only the hulking brute possessed the strength necessary to bruise his body even through the backpack he'd worn at the time.

Blade gazed off to his right at the thicket screening Geronimo and again to his left at the base of a tree where

Hickok lay hidden. Neither one was visible.

His simple plan called for staying concealed until either the mysterious wood nymphs or someone from the castle put in an appearance. If the former showed up, he'd try to capture one. If Morlock or Elphinstone appeared, he'd wait and see what they did before deciding on a course of action.

Cradling the Marlin in his arms, he settled down to spend the night if need be.

Blade mentally reviewed his performance in the castle and concluded he had a lot to learn yet about being a Warrior. He never should have gone after Endora by himself or let her lure him into an ambush. The mistake might have proven fatal.

And there was another mystery. Given Morlock's hatred of outsiders, and since, as Morlock claimed, he believed his wife was being attacked, why did Morlock use a net and a chair instead of a gun or knives?

There were so many questions and so few answers.

Another full moon arced above the horizon, a timeless celestial observer of the unfolding of human history.

An hour went by. Two.

Blade half-expected there wouldn't be activity of any kind until near midnight, so he was surprised when, idly glancing to the southwest, he spied pale figures gliding through the trees toward the camp.

The nymphs!

Excited, he tensed and watched the three or four dozen creatures rapidly near his position. They were tittering and prancing, the same as last night, remarkably light on their feet. He marveled at their grace and ghostly aspect, keeping as still as stone until they were almost to the oak tree.

Recognition brought shock. Blade's gray eyes narrowed as he realized they were human, near-naked men and women whose skin resembled the finest china. They were all over six feet tall but skinny as saplings. Members of both sexes wore skimpy leather shorts, nothing else, and the womens' breasts swayed as they ran. All were grinning or whispering excitedly.

Blade focused on a pair almost directly below him, a man and a woman standing a foot apart. He quietly looped the Marlin over his right shoulder, coiled his legs and leaped.

Somehow, the woman sensed his presence and looked up.

The youth landed behind them, bending at the knees to absorb his weight, and sprang, tackling both of them around the legs and bearing them to the ground. They felt incredibly light, as if they weighed a mere 90 or 100 pounds, and offered no resistance except for a startled cry from the woman.

At the same time Hickok and Geronimo rose from hiding and tried to capture others, but the rest of the band was already fleeing in stark panic into the forest.

Blade lay on top of the two he'd caught, neither of whom so much as twitched, astounded by their docile behavior. "I won't hurt you," he informed them. "Do you understand?"

There was no reply.

"Do you understand?" Blade repeated sternly.

"We do," the woman said in a high, musical voice.

"Shhhhh," said the man. "You know we're not allowed to talk to outers."

Perplexed, Blade eased his grip. "All right. You speak English. Good. Now listen closely. I'm going to sit up and let go of you. First I want your word that you won't try to escape."

"We can't give it, sir," the woman said.

"Why not?"

"Because our masts have told us we must get away if ever we're caught by outers."

The man looked at the woman. "Hush, Tabitha, you know better."

Blade clamped a hand on a wrist of each one and rose to his knees. "Okay. If you won't give your word, we'll do this the hard way." He stood, pulling them up, but being careful not to yank too hard for fear of yanking their arms from their sockets. "What's your name?" he asked the male.

The man said nothing.

"Tell me or else," Blade bluffed, glowering appropriately.

"Selwyn," the man blurted. "My name is Selwyn."

Blade glanced over his left shoulder and saw his friends returning empty-handed from the chase. "Come with me," he said, walking toward the camp.

Both prisoners abruptly walked, dragging their heels and tugging in vain to free themselves.

"Please, sir, no," Tabitha exclaimed.

"Not near the fire," Selwyn stated in sheer dread.

"Why not?" Blade demanded, stopping.

"The fire hurts our eyes terribly, sir," Selwyn said. "If we get too close, the brightness will damage our eyes."

"It's only a campfire," Blade noted.

"Our eyes are very sensitive, sir," Tabitha explained. "We can't even come out during the day."

Her plaintive tone impressed Blade. He studied their fine features, their straw-colored hair and almost colorless eyes, and realized the reason they were so pale. They spent their entire life in the dark, moving about only at night. But what did they do during the day? Where did they live? "Don't worry," he assured them. "I won't take you any nearer to the fire."

"Thank you, sir. You're very kind," Tabitha said.

The gunfighter and the Blackfoot halted and regarded the pair intently.

"I'm sorry, pard," Hickok said. "I'll never doubt your word again. These things are livin' fairies, just like you said."

"We are not things, sir," Tabitha declared. "We are serfs."

"Serfs," Hickok repeated. "Like back in the Middle Ages?"

"What are the Middle Ages, sir?" Tabitha asked.

"It was back in ancient times when men wore tin cans into battle and women went around throwin' their hair from balconies."

Tabitha and Selwyn were completely confounded.

"How did women throw their hair, sir?" she asked.

"Pay no attention to him," Geronimo interjected. "His grasp of history leaves a lot to be desired."

"Where did you acquire the name serfs?" Blade probed.

"I don't know, sir," Tabitha responded. "We've always been called serfs, I believe. My mother and her mother were both serfs. And for our lives we serve our masts loyally."

"There's that word again. Who are the masts?"

"Why, those who provide our clothes, our home and the food. They are the great ones who know all there is to know," Tabitha said, then added quickly, "sir."

"Do you mean masters?" Geronimo asked.

"Masts. Masters. They're the same thing, sir."

"It's slang," Blade realized, wondering what to inquire about next. "You say your people have been serving your masters for generations. Who are your masts?"

"Like I said, sir, the great ones."

"Where do the great ones live?"

Tabitha nodded at the castle. "Why, there, sir, in the great house."

The three youths exchanged meaningful looks.

"So Morlock, Endora and Elphinstone are the masters," Blade said slowly.

"Oh, yes!" Tabitha declared. "Master Morlock is the greatest of all."

Selwyn made a clucking sound. "And he will be very

mad if he learns you are telling these outers all about us."

The statement produced stark fear on Tabitha's face. "But what else can I do?"

"Don't worry about Morlock," Blade told her. "We'll make sure he doesn't do anything to you for talking to us."

"Do you know him, sir?"

"Yes. In fact, we were guests in the great house today," Blade stated, stretching the truth in order to elicit more information.

"You were, sir?" Tabitha said, delighted at the news. "Why, then, you must not be outers after all."

"What the dickens are outers?" Hickok asked.

"Outsiders, sir, such as yourself."

"You mean those who come from outside this valley?" Blade asked.

"Exactly, sir. Only we call this valley the Domain."

"Have there been outers in the Domain before?"

"Yes, sir. Every now and then some have shown up."

"Did they stay long?"

"I wouldn't know, sir. Usually they are invited into the great house, and we never see or hear of them again."

Blade frowned. Yet another sinister revelation to add to the growing body of evidence incriminating Morlock and his clan. How long had all of this been going on? Since the war? He now had proof that some force of slavery was being practiced, and slavery was abhorrent to every cherished principle of the Family. As a Warrior, he had a moral obligation to confront evil wherever it reared its wicked head, and from all he'd uncovered so far it was flourishing in Castle Orm.

"Now would you please let us go, sir?" Tabitha requested. "Our masts will be very upset with us if we don't get to work soon."

"Work?"

"Yes, sir. In the fields. Every night they let us out to till the crops and weed and water the garden."

Suddenly several mysteries were cleared up. All those naked footprints were left by the serfs as they went about their noctural business at the beck and call of Morlock and company. And so many crops were being cultivated because the food had to feed all the serfs, not just the freaky threesome in the castle. One of her comments, though, perplexed him. "Where do the serfs live during the day?"

"In the Underground, sir."

"Where might that be?"

"In the levels under the great house, sir."

Another puzzle cleared up, Blade reflected. The reason Endora confronted them on the stairs was to prevent them from descending farther into the levels where the serfs lived. "When we were in the great house today, we happaned to hear someone screaming and wailing. Do you know who that was?"

Sorrow etched the faces of both serfs.

"Yes, sir," Tabitha said. "That was poor Tweena. Master Elphinstone punished her for coming back here by herself last night."

"Explain."

"When we spotted your campfire last night, all of us came for a look when Grell went off to relieve himself. You saw us and we hid. Remember, sir?"

"I remember," Blade said. "But who is Grell? We haven't met him yet."

Selwyn shuddered and gazed into the surrounding darkness. "You don't want to meet him, sir. He's the immortal one."

Blade was confused again. "Skip him for the moment. Tell me about Tweena."

"She wanted to sneak back for a second look, sir," Tabitha explained. "We tried to talk her out of it, but she went anyway, alone. You spotted her and chased her to the portal, and Master Morlock caught her. Naturally, the great ones saw fit to punish her."

"They did, huh?"

"Oh, yes sir. They found out that all of us snuck away for a peek at you and decided to teach us the error of our ways by using Tweena as an example."

The statement rang false in Blade's ears. He suspected she was quoting words spoken by one of the great masters, probably Morlock. "What did they do to Tweena?"

Tabitha lowered her gaze and spoke in a whisper. "Horrible things, sir. Grell, Master Elphinstone and Master Morlock all took turns, beating and torturing her." She paused. "Tweena is in heaven now."

"They made us watch, sir," Selwyn said. "It was the most terrible thing I've ever seen, even worse than the time Grell ate Cathmor."

Blade wasn't certain he'd heard correctly. "This Grell ate one of the serfs?"

"Yes, sir. Cathmor tried to leave the Domain, and that's strictly forbidden by our masts."

"What the heck have we stumbled into?" Hickok spoke up. "Who ever heard of killin' a woman for takin' a look at strangers? And folks eatin' other folks is downright sick."

Geronimo fixed his eyes on Blade's. "You know what we have to do, don't you?"

"Yes."

"We can't let these atrocities continue."

"I know."

Hickok nodded. "Now you're really talkin'. Let's go find Morlock so I can shove both Colt barrels up his nose and see if his noggin is bulletproof."

"First things first," Blade said, turning to Tabitha. "There's something I don't understand. If Tweena was punished to keep the serfs away from our camp, why did all of you return tonight?"

The dainty woman's mood changed from sadness to giddy elation in the space of a heartbeat. She giggled and stated proudly, "We wanted to see you again. Grell heard an animal in the woods and went to check if it was dangerous. He protects us, you see, sir."

"And eats you," Blade reminded her. "But go on."

"As soon as he was out of sight, we dropped our tools and ran over here. We expected to be back before he returned. We're much faster than Grell, sir."

"And eats you," Blade reminded her. "But go on."

"And what about Tweena? Didn't her death impress you at all?"

"Yes, sir. It was horrible. I told you so."

"Yet all the serfs came anyway?"

Tabitha giggled again. "We like to break the rules. It's fun."

The inane smile creasing the woman's thin lips gave Blade cause for concern. "In other words, none of the serfs were fazed one bit by Tweena's death?"

"Not really, sir. No."

"When Cathmor was eaten, how did you feel about it?"

"Well, sir, the masts only did it to teach us a lesson. And they teach us lessons because they love us."

Hickok snorted. "Did I miss something here?"

Before anyone else could speak, a tremendous roar shattered the stillness of the forest, a roar the three youths had heard during their first night in the woods.

"It's Grell!" Tabitha screeched.

CHAPTER TWELVE

So stunned was Blade by the ferocious sound, he froze. In his mind's eye he saw the enormous creature with the glowing red eyes and felt again a tingle of fear ripple down his spine. He inadvertently released his hold on the serfs and gripped his Bowies.

Tabitha and Selwyn were off like panic-stricken antelope, bounding to the northwest in airy leaps.

"Run, sirs!" Tabitha cried.

"What *do* we do?" Geronimo inquired, the Winchester molded to his shoulder.

Blade wanted to answer, but couldn't. His lips wouldn't respond to his mental commands, and his body was frozen in place. Even his heart seemed to have stopped. He gaped in the direction of the roar, to the southwest, and experienced an almost overwhelming impulse to run.

"I say we show it who's boss," Hickok suggested, drawing the Colts.

"Are you crazy? Didn't you see how big that thing was last night?" Geronimo responded.

"Hey, the bigger they are, the harder they fall."

Sensation returned to Blade's limbs. He gulped and slid both knives from their sheaths. His heart hadn't stopped beating after all because now it was thumping in his chest and the veins in his temples were pounding, his entire body pulsing vibrantly, an adrenaline rush to end all adenaline rushes making every nerve and muscle, every tiny cell, quiver expectantly. But this wasn't the pleasant rush brought on by intimacy with a loved one, nor the giddy rush of facing foes bravely in a battle to the death. This was a perverse rush, a rush he'd never known of outright cowardice. For the very first time in his young life Blade felt genuinely afraid of an adversary. Fear was an alien experience until that very moment, and being alien it tore down his psychlogical defenses and left him spiritually naked, his soul in supreme turmoil.

Hickok glanced at his giant friend and did an exaggerated double take. "What's with you, pard? You look sick."

Licking his dry lips, Blade opened his mouth to reply when he saw it, saw the monster, the thing moving directly toward them from out of the gloom. Ten feet high, its reddish eyes radiating malevolence, the creature effortlessly barged through the undergrowth, the thump-thump-thump of its feet growing louder and louder, matching the thump-thump-thump of Blade's heart.

"Are you okay, Blade?" Geronimo asked.

"Yeah," Blade mumbled.

"Since you want to be the boss on this expedition of yours, do we fight or what?" Hickok inquired.

The creature was close enough now to reveal its thick reddish coat of fur, its stout legs the size of tree trunks and its massive arms.

Blade couldn't stand to look into those red eyes any longer. "Let's take cover until it leaves," he proposed, backing up.

"You want to *run*?" Hickok declared in astonishment.

"We don't know what we're up against. Until we do,

let's play it safe."

"Some Warrior you'll turn out to be."

The monstrosity was only 30 feet away.

"We can argue later," Blade snapped. "Let's go." Whirling, he raced toward their camp, feeling deeply ashamed of his decision and suspecting his friends sensed the truth. He stopped at the campsite to grab his backpack. A glance over his shoulder showed the beast known as Grell lumbering in pursuit. Elation coursed through him, replacing the fear, when he saw it couldn't move faster than a ponderous walk. We can easily outrun it, he thought, and laughed.

"What's so funny, pard," Hickok asked, lifting his backpack.

"Nothing."

"If you don't mind my sayin' so, I think the beating you took rattled your brain. You're not actin' like your normal self."

Ignoring the comment, Blade started northward. "Come on. Let's get out of there."

"Why not?" Hickok grumbled. "We seem to be makin' it a habit to turn yellow at the first sign of danger."

Blade led them at a dogtrot for 40 yards, than halted and gazed at their camp.

The monster was nearly there. Grell stepped close to the fire, unaffected by the bright flames, and snarled in frustration. He proceeded to rip the lean-to into kindling with powerful swipes of his huge paws, then tramped on the broken bits for added measure. Finished, he glared at the youths and roared his defiance.

"*Please* let me plug the varmint," Hickok begged.

"Not yet."

"When? Next year?"

Blade saw Grell depart, heading toward the castle, and he was tempted to charge, to try and kill the thing in a hail of lead. But what if the bullets had no effect? To a creature that massive a gunshot might be equivalent to a bee sting, and if their guns proved useless, what then? Did he want to face it with just his Bowies? The answer was no. "Let's see if we can find the serfs," he suggested. "There are still a lot of questions they need to answer."

"Lead the way," Geronimo said.

Hickok vented a protracted sigh while watching the monster crash through the brush. "Sure. Whatever you want, pard."

Taking a few seconds to orient himself by using the stars, Blade hiked in the directions of the tilled field and the garden. He felt uncomfortable at leaving without making at least a token effort to slay Grell, but he couldn't bring himself to turn around and go back.

"That thing is the biggest mutation I've ever seen or heard of," Geronimo commented. "I wonder how Morlock exerts control over it?"

"Most likely with his charming personality," Hickok quipped.

"Why do you think Selwyn referred to it as the immortal one?" Geronimo wondered.

"Who knows?" Hickok rejoined. "I don't make it a habit of tryin' to figure out fruit loops and fairies."

"They're serfs, remember?"

"Serfs, smerfs, what's the difference?"

They walked in silence for five minutes, listening to the receding footsteps of the monster.

"I had no idea mutations grew so big," Geronimo said.

"Drop the subject, will you?" Blade snapped. "We have other things to consider."

"Like what, pard?"

"Like what we're going to do about Morlock, Endora and Elphinstone."

"What's to consider? We blow 'em away."

"I agree we must stop them from enslaving the serfs,

but how far can we go? Do we have the right to kill them, if need be?''

''Sure we do,'' Hickok said without hesitation.

''Oh? Even though they're not a threat to the Family?''

''What's that got to do with anything?''

''Everything,'' Blade said. ''You and I are Warriors. We're pledged to safeguard the Home. Technically speaking, neither of us has jurisdiction here.''

Hickok chuckled. ''Why worry about a measly thing like jurisdiction when it comes to blowin' away a couple of lowlifes?''

''Because if we kill Morlock or any member of his family without proper justification, we're no better than common killers. Morally, we'd be in the wrong.''

''Here you go with the morality business again. Why don't you forget being a Warrior and become a spiritual Teacher instead?''

The sarcastic comment stung Blade. A few years ago he *had* toyed with the idea of becoming a Teacher, as the Family designated those gifted individuals who possessed the capacity to teach truth and were in tune with the Source of all, but he'd decided his natural talents lay elsewhere.

Except for an occasional insect noise and once the hooting of an owl, an eerie stillness enveloped the forest.

Blade hoped his sense of direction was equal to the task and received confirmation when they broke from the trees and discovered the garden straight ahead. There was no sign of the serfs. ''Where are they?'' he absently mumbled.

''Probably off huggin' trees,'' Hickok said.

''They could have heard us coming and ran off,'' Geronimo guessed.

They skirted the garden until they came to the grassy road. Parked there was a crudely constructed, wooden wagon, six feet high and with immense wooden wheels and a thick beam for a tongue. Tilling implements were piled high inside.

"So now we know what made the ruts," Geronimo observed.

"Maybe they went to the castle," Blade said. "Let's check." Only when he uttered the recommendation did he recall Grell had headed toward the castle. Again he thought of the enormous brute and those eyes the color of fresh blood, and he involuntarily shivered as if from a chilling breeze. It was too late to change his mind without arousing suspicion, so he led them slowly along the road.

The front of the castle came into sight and with it the narrow field in front where dozens of pale forms danced and played in innocent abandon.

"Get down," Blade whispered, dropping to one knee.

"What the blazes are they doing now?" Hickok asked.

"Having fun," Geronimo said.

"With that hairy fart runnin' around loose? Those people ain't playin' with a full deck, if you get my drift."

"They're like children," Geronimo remarked quietly. "I'd say they have the emotional maturity of twelve year-olds."

"Should we try to capture one again?"

"Not yet," Blade answered. "They'd see us and take off. We're no match for them unless we can take them by surprise."

"Now I've heard everything," Hickok complained. "When you wouldn't let us tangle with Morlock and that great ape earlier, I held my peace. And when you beat a retreat without takin' on Grell, I figured you knew what you were doing." He gestured at the serfs. "But when you claim we're no match for a bunch of bimbos and dorks who like to traipse around in their underwear and who couldn't stomp a flea in a fair fight, I draw the line." So saying, the gunfighter rose and sped toward the serfs.

"Wait," Blade said. He tried to grab his friend's wrist and missed. He saw the pale figures collectively whirl around and gape at Hickok, then they fled en masse, giggling and running without really exerting themselves.

The gunfighter never slowed.

"Damn," Blade snapped and took off after him.

Geronimo kept pace on the giant's left. "You'll have to forgive Nathan," he commented.

"Why should I?" Blade responded testily.

"Because unlike the rest of us, he gets by with half a brain."

"When I'm done with him, he won't even have that."

Predictably, the serfs reached the castle well ahead of their puffing pursuer and ran along the base of the wall toward the yard in back.

The gunfighter was doing his best, but it was the tortoise and the hare all over again, and he wasn't the hare.

"Hickok! Stop!" Blade bellowed, and when his cry produced no result, added under his breath, "Idiot."

"You've got to admit there's never a dull moment with him around," Geronimo said proudly.

"For someone who's always on his case, you certainly stick up for him a lot."

"What are friends for?"

Blade increased his pace, annoyed that he wouldn't be able to overtake Hickok before the gunfighter reached the rear corner. He didn't like the idea of Hickok being out of sight, even for ten seconds. "Will you stop?" he shouted.

Incredibly, Hickok glanced back and grinned, his white teeth contrasted by the darkness. "I'm gainin'," he replied and kept going.

"Remind me to dunk him in the moat when we get back," Blade said angrily.

"Okay."

"Fifty or sixty times."

In graceful leaps and bounds the serfs went around the castle and disappeared.

"Hickok, don't—" Blade began and stopped in midcry

when the gunfighter took the corner. He pumped his arms and legs frantically, pulling ahead of Geronimo, and pounded into the rear yard with his mouth open to chew out Hickok for being such a blockhead.

But Hickok wasn't there.

Nor were the serfs.

Stunned, Blade halted so abruptly he nearly tripped over his own feet. He glanced to the right and the left. It was impossible, and yet it had happened. His intuitive dread had not been unfounded.

Geronimo came around the corner and stopped short. "Where's Nathan?" he blurted.

"You tell me," Blade said, gazing at the castle and the mausoleums, and jogged toward the latter when the thought occurred to him that Hickok might be behind one of the tombs.

Geronimo ran at his side. "He couldn't have just vanished," he declared in astonishment.

"He did."

They conducted a sweep of the mausoleums but found no trace of their rash companion. Winding up in front of the biggest tomb, they stood in mutual, baffled contemplation, trying to make sense of the inexplicable.

"Maybe they kept going around to the other side of the castle," Geronimo conjectured. "I'll go see." He sprinted off.

Blade idly stared at the Blackfoot, thinking they must stay there until daylight and scour the ground for tracks, expecting him to stop at the southeast corner. He never thought to advise Geronimo to stay in sight and was extremely upset when his friend pulled a Hickok and ran around to the east side. "Geronimo!" he called out, starting forward, his gaze straying to the castle.

Standing at a third floor window, her white dress impossible to miss, was Endora.

"Geronimo!" Blade repeated, louder this time, his

intuition flaring again, and when no response was forthcoming, he raced to the corner and stopped in breathless bewilderment.

The stretch of ground between the southeast and northeast corners was empty.

Geronimo, like the gunfighter, had disappeared.

CHAPTER THIRTEEN

He was alone!

Blade backed against the wall, the Marlin leveled, his heart beating wildly again, his temples drumming. He gulped and scrutinized the forest, half-expecting to see those savage red orbs glaring at him.

It couldn't be!

They couldn't both vanish.

He blinked and stepped into the yard, swinging the rifle first one way, then another, his nerves raw, itching to fire at anything that moved. His face was clammy with sweat despite the cool breeze. His mind was a blank slate. Dazed, he walked to the big mausoleum and crouched beside it. Endora was no longer visible in the window.

Get a grip, damn you!

Blade shook his head, confused by his reaction. He'd never been afraid of anything before, but the monster known as Grell had terrified him—and now this! What was happening to him? Maybe he wasn't cut out to be a Warrior. Maybe he didn't have what it took, didn't possess true courage. He'd never been tested in combat or faced such a grim predicament. This was his first real crisis, and he was cracking under the strain.

What should he do?

Breathing deeply, he willed himself to calm down and relax, controlling his emotions. A Warrior should always maintain strict self-control. That was the beginning lesson taught by the Elder responsible for training novice Warriors. Superb self-control was the foundation on which rested all other attributes essential to a Warrior.

Next came dedication, loyalty to a higher ideal, and in his case it was the ideal represented by the Home and the Family, the ideal of love and stability realized by the descendants of Kurt Carpenter. On a practical level, he was glad to be able to serve the Family by protecting them from any and all threats to their continued survival.

Also critically important to any Warrior was an acceptance of the inevitable. Everyone died. Sooner or later everyone passed on to the higher mansions. Death was simply the means of throwing off the earthly coil and ascending to the next level. Warriors, more so than most, must resign themselves to the fact they lived with a heightened prospect of death every single day. Dying was an ever-present consequence of living a life devoted to safeguarding others and confronting lethal dangers on a daily basis.

Was that his problem?

Hadn't he learned to accept the inevitability of death?

Why else did he fear the mutation so much?

The revelation sparked profound thought, and Blade leaned on the mausoleum, totally oblivious to the passage of time, while he pondered the ramifications. Sure, he didn't want to die, but then who did? By the same token, he didn't want his friends to die either. And if he didn't get his act together, they surely would.

What was the key to solving his problem? How could he find the courage to confront Grell? Where did true courage spring from, anyway? The heart? The mind? The personality? Or a combination of all three. What distinguished a man labeled brave from one branded a coward? Why were some men able to face death without flinching while others fled pell-mell? More to the point, which kind of man was he?

Which did he want to be?

Naturally, he wanted to be brave. Although only 16, he had adult responsibilities, and it was time he started owning up to them. He must conquer his fear and save his comrades.

Easier said than done.

How do you conquer fear? Blade asked himself. How do you overcome an intangible emotional state? Facing the object of one's fears was supposed to work, but he'd already faced Grell twice and quaked both times. If he could change his attitude, he'd be able to take on the mutation without flinching.

How did someone change their attitude?

The heart and mind alone couldn't do it, but the personality could through force of will. Was that the answer? Something so basic as willpower, the simple matter of making up one's mind? If a person wanted to be happy, all they had to do was will themselves to believe they were happy despite whatever external circumstances prevailed. Therefore, if someone wanted to be brave, all they had to do was believe they were brave.

Was that the way it worked?

Could so crucial a quality be so easy to obtain?

Shaking his head to clear his thoughts, Blade rose and scanned the yard and the castle. He'd worry about his problem later. Right now Hickok and Geronimo were more important. He took a step toward the castle, intending to start his search on the east side, when a scraping noise from the front of the mausoleum made him dart back. He peeked around the corner, his eyes widening in surprise.

The recessed front door was sliding open.

Elphinstone suddenly emerged.

Blade jerked his head from view, waited a few seconds, then risked another look.

The apish brute was pressing on one of the etched figures to the right of the door. Almost soundlessly the opening swung closed. Turning, Elphinstone walked to the northwest and disappeared around the corner.

Where was he going? Blade wondered. He stepped to the entrance and examined the walls on both sides. Carved into the marble near the right jamb was a reproduction of the crest engraved near the top of the tomb—the man in armor holding the head and body of a child. That had to be the one. Tentatively, he reached out and pressed on the cool surface, and to his delight the door moved inward on well-oiled hinges.

A quick check verified no one was watching. Blade ducked inside, then paused. There must be a way to close the door from within. He found himself on a spiral metal staircase that descended into the bowels of the earth. All below was pitch black.

Blade hesitated. Grell might be down there—but so might his friends. He felt the wall for a figure, switch or lever, but found none. Leaving the door open was his only option. Taking hold of the rail, he slowly headed down, treading carefully, wary of tripping and plunging to a hard floor far below.

Doubts assailed him. What good could he do if he couldn't see three feet in front of his face? He'd be easy prey for anyone—or anything—lurking in the lower levels. But if he turned back now he might as well keep going all the way to the Home. He'd never be able to look anyone else in the eyes again. Of all the shameful acts men committed, few rivaled deserting friends in an hour of need.

His soles scraped softly on the steps, and in his nervous state he was certain the noise could be heard for hundreds of feet. He breathed shallowly, straining his ears, and glanced upward every few seconds to see if he was being followed.

The staircase seemed to go on forever.

Blade estimated he'd desended 100 feet when he reached the bottom and discerned the outline of a corridor extending to the north, toward the castle. Stepping to the right-hand wall, he placed his palm on the smooth stone and continued onward. The familiar dank smell permeated the air.

For 20 yards the corridor ran straight without a break, and then a junction signified he'd arrived at the levels under the castle. Blade scanned each branch and elected to go forward. His eyes had adjusted to the murky conditions sufficiently for him to discriminate doorways on both sides.

All the doors were closed. He tried the first one on the left and found it locked. The next door on the right was likewise secure. But the third door opened at the twisting of its knob and revealed a huge storeroom beyond.

Blade slid in and surveyed shelves piled high with goods, stacks of crates and boxes, and tables laden with all kinds of articles. Conducting a closer examination, he discovered a stash of canned goods in the southwest corner, and by holding the cans up to his face he was able to read those labels bearing white print. There were peaches, fruit cocktail, string beans, lima beans, corn, several types of juice, zucchini and much more. From the dust covering them, he guessed the cans had been placed there almost 100 years ago by Moray, the first lord of Castle Orm.

He found tools, untouched medical supplies, piles of clothing, blankets, and even pots and pans. None of the goods gave evidence of use, which puzzled him. Why had Moray's ancestors let all this stuff go to waste? Perhaps for the very same reason the Family hadn't used all the supplies stockpiled by the Founder; it would take 1000 years to do so. Both men, apparently, provided more than their descendants would need for many, many generations to come.

A cabinet in a corner arrested his attention. He opened a door and found the equivalent of a gold mine in the form of three boxes of matches. Eagerly he scooped them up, placed two in his pockets and opened the third. Now all he needed to do—

What was that?

Blade stiffened at the faint patter of footsteps in the passageway. Crouching, he aimed at the doorway.

A pale figure appeared, then another.

"Pard, are you in here?"

Blade recognized Tabitha's voice. Flabbergasted, he rose and moved into the open. "Tabitha and Selwyn?"

"Yep," the woman replied happily.

"This isn't my idea, sir," Selwyn stated quickly. "She made me do it." He sighed. "The things brothers do for their sisters."

The youth walked over to them. "I don't understand. What are you doing here?"

"We've been following you, sir," Tabitha said.

"Following me?"

"Yes, sir. Ever since Grell came. We hid in the forest and watched him destroy your camp, then we followed after you."

"I thought you'd rejoined the other serfs."

"Not yet, Pard. We're having too much fun."

Blade looked into her pale eyes. "Why do you keep calling me pard?"

"Isn't that your name, sir? We heard the blond one call you Pard."

"My name is Blade."

"Oh. We're sorry, sir."

Blade leaned closer. "Tell me. Did you happen to see what happened to my friends?"

"No, sir," Tabitha answered.

"We did see Master Elphinstone going toward the front

of the great house,'' Selwyn disclosed and giggled. ''He never saw us hiding in the weeds.''

A frown creased Blade's lips. There it was again, a hint of immaturity or instability or a combination of both. The serfs knew they would be punished for their transgressions, yet they viewed the whole affair as a great game. ''Why have you been following me?''

''Because we like you, sir,'' Tabitha said.

''Please call me Blade.''

''Okay. Because we like you, Blade, sir.''

''Do you know where we are?''

''Of course, sir. In the lowest level below the great house. There are a lot of rooms with many strange things in them, just like this one.''

''More storerooms?''

''More rooms like this one, sir.''

''On which level do the serfs live?''

''The next two up.''

''Take me there.''

''If you want, sir, but Master Morlock and Mistress Endora might be there. They'll punish us,'' Selwyn said.

''Take me.''

Brother and sister turned and exited the room.

Cramming the third box of matches into a back pocket, Blade trailed them. He'd save the box until it was really needed. They passed more doors and once a branch to the right. ''Where does that go?'' he inquired.

''The bone room, sir,'' Tabitha said. ''It's where Grell throws the bones of all the animals and such he eats.''

The mention of the monster quickened Blade's pulse, but he didn't allow the panic to seize control again. ''He saves bones?''

''Yes, sir. Likes to munch on them when the masts give him time to himself. The room is sort of his den.''

''Keep going.''

The serfs guided the youth to the central stairway and started up the steps. They slowed when they were halfway to the next landing and turned to the giant.

"We'd rather not go any farther, sir," Tabithaa said respectfully.

"That's right, Blade, sir," Selwyn started. "We're just not in the mood to be punished right now. We'd rather stay out until morning and take our medicine then."

"You don't need to worry. I won't let any of your masts harm you."

"I doubt you can persuade them not to punish us, sir," Tabitha said.

"There are ways."

Shrugging, the pair climbed higher.

Blade followed and could make out the landing and several forks. It wasn't pitch black, after all, and he attributed the reason to moonlight filtering in from outdoors. The matches would help, but any light on the lower levels would undoubtedly attract Morlock and company like a campfire in the open sometimes attracted murderous scavengers.

They reached the landing and halted, Tabitha and Selwyn hanging back, reluctant to advance.

"Please let us leave, sir," she begged.

"You have nothing to fear," Blade told them. He walked to the left-hand fork and peered down the corridor, then turned his back to the middle branch and smiled at his newfound friends. "I'll take care of you."

An express train hurtled out of the darkness and slammed into his back.

CHAPTER FOURTEEN

The impact knocked Blade prone, the breath whooshing from his lungs, and sent the Marlin skidding across the landing. He heard Tabitha and Selwyn laugh—laugh?—and then he frantically pushed to his knees and tried to turn. A naked foot caught him at the base of the neck and sent him down again, his surroundings spinning as if in a whirlpool.

The serfs laughed below.

Numb from the last blow, Blade feebly attempted to roll over. Iron hands closed on his shoulders, and he was bodily lifted into the air. He struggled weakly, but it wasn't enough to prevent his assailant from throwing him against a corridor wall. He landed on his left side and finally saw his attacker.

The hulking form of Elphinstone moved toward the youth, his mallet-like hands clenched into huge fists.

In a certain sense, Blade felt relieved. It was the apish brute, not Grell. At least he stood a chance. Since he'd arrived at Castle Orm, he'd been played a fool, beaten, treated like dirt, and experienced the supreme humiliation of stark cowardice. Now was his chance to show these bastards what Warriors were made of.

Elphinstone halted next to the youth's head and leaned down to grab him.

Not this time, Blade thought, driving his knees up and around, his legs bent, and succeeding in catching Elphinstone in the left temple.

The brute grunted and staggered backward.

Blade was up in a flash, in the on-guard stance. He considered resorting to his Bowies and promptly discarded the notion. His foe wasn't armed. Using the knives would be unfair.

Neither of the serfs were laughing.

Straightening, Elphinstone vented an inarticulate growl and charged, swinging his fists wildly, going for the youth's face.

This time Blade was ready. He ducked under a couple of punches that would have caved in his skull and delivered three swift jabs to the brute's ribs. When Elphinstone shifted to the right, Blade pivoted, pressing his initiative, burying his left fist in the apish man's stomach and following through with a right to the jaw that rocked Elphinstone on his heels.

Instantly, Blade closed in, kneeing his adversary in the groin. Elphinstone wheezed and doubled over, and Blade executed a flawless snap kick into the brute's nose that sent him tottering backward almost to the edge of the landing. "Had enough?" he asked.

Elphinstone recovered his balance and bellowed his enraged response. "No!"

Blade wanted to end the fight before Morlock or Grell showed up, especially Grell. As Elphinstone came toward him, he ran to meet the brute halfway. But instead of using his fists, he leaped into the air, performing a flying side kick, the yoko-tobi-geri, and struck Elphinstone full in the mouth.

As if smashed by a sledgehammer, Elphinstone catapulted head over heels onto his stomach with a loud thud. For a moment he lay stunned. His head slowly rose from the hard floor, his lips cracked and bleeding, and he spat blood. With a guttural growl, he started to rise.

Blade was ready. Instead of slugging it out with the brute, he must rely on the martial arts. Elphinstone obviously knew nothing of the science of self-defense, and while the brute might be stronger, his reflexes and coordination were no match for Blade's.

The young Warrior glided in and flicked a snap kick to his foe's head before Elphinstone could rise, rocking the apish man on his haunches. Another snap kick with the right leg was blocked, but a crescent kick with the left connected and sent the brute onto his back.

Elphinstone took longer to rise this time. Dark stains coated the lower half of his face and neck. He grunted as he propped himself on his elbows, then came off the floor in a surprising burst of speed.

Still in the on-guard stance, Blade retreated a step to give himself more room and leaped into the air, whipping his body in a spinning back kick that hit the brute at the base of the throat and lifted Elphinstone from his feet to sail to the edge of the landing and over it. He alighted on the balls of his feet and moved to the first step, expecting to see the apish figure barreling up toward him.

There was no one there.

Perplexed, Blade scanned the stairs below and saw no sign of his adversary. Yet Elphinstone had to be down there, somewhere. He doubted the brute was gravely injured. It would take more than a few kicks to put the Neanderthal out of commission. Pivoting, he looked at the serfs.

Tabitha and Selwyn were riveted in place, their expressions reflecting total astonishment.

Blade anticipated they would be elated at his victory

and walked up to them. "See? I told you I'd take care of you."

"You hurt him!" Tabitha declared angrily. "You hurt Master Elphinstone!"

"You had no right to be so cruel!" Selwyn added.

Bewildered by their passionate reaction, Blade blinked and jabbed a finger at the stairs. "He was trying to kill me," he said defensively.

"He was not," Tabitha disagreed. "He probably just wanted to put you in a cage."

"And you think I should have let him?"

"Certainly. He's one of the masts, after all. All of us should serve them gladly."

"I'm no one's slave," Blade snapped, "and I don't serve your masts. If I can, I'm going to put them out of business for good."

"What do you mean, sir?"

"I mean I'm going to put an end to their enslavement of the serfs."

The brother and sister looked at each other.

"You can't," Selwyn responded in horror, forgetting his usual excessive civility.

In exasperation Blade threw his hands into the air and both serfs flinched. "Why not?" he demanded.

"Who will watch over us?" Tabitha asked, on the verge of tears. "Who will protect us and clothe us and feed us?"

The implications of her questions shook Blade to the core of his being. He took a pace backward and gazed at them in blatant disbelief. "Let me get this straight. You *want* them to take care of you?"

"Of course, sir," Tabitha said.

"'We'd be lost without them, sir," Selwyn chimed in.

"But they take advantage of you."

Tabitha giggled. "How do they ever do that, sir?"

"They make you work for them, make you till the fields to produce their food, and they keep you cooped up during the day. You're little better than slaves."

"Oh, you have it all wrong, sir. We like working for the masts. They love us and treat us fairly."

"How can you say such a thing? They beat and tortured your friend Tweena until she died. And Grell *ate* a serf."

Tabitha nodded. "But Tweena deserved to be punished for disobeying the masts. And Cathmor deserved to be eaten for trying to leave the Domain."

The absurd illogic baffled Blade, and he pressed a palm to his forehead as he tried to make sense of it all. The serfs were enslaved and didn't even know it. Worse, they preferred the status quo. How could they? Didn't they realize how precious freedom was?

"Can we go now, sir?" Tabitha asked.

"Go where?" Blade responded absently.

"We'd like to find our friends and play before dawn, sir," Selwyn said.

"Or before the masts catch us," Tabitha stated and snickered.

Blade stared at their pale skin, at their pale features, at their pale eyes, and suddenly their very paleness offended him. Their personalities were as colorless as their complexions, devoid of all character, stripped of any semblance of conviction and independence. They were pale imitations of human beings, at best, puppets on a string who didn't want the puppeteers removed. "Go," he said harshly. "Get out of here."

The serfs giggled and danced down the stairs, and moments later they were swallowed by the inky shadows.

Good riddance, Blade reflected. He abruptly realized his rifle was missing and scoured the landing until he found it. As he stooped to retreive the Marlin he heard a little laugh behind him.

"I could have spared you a lot of trouble, boy."

Startled, Blade crouched and spun, leveling the rifle, his finger on the trigger. He saw the thin figure of the lord of Castle Orm standing at the junction.

"I'm unarmed," Morlock said calmly.

The youth hesitated, suspecting a trick. "Don't move or I'll shoot."

"There's no need for violence, boy."

"The name is Blade, remember? Come closer so I can see you."

Morlock advanced and held out his empty hands to demonstrate he posed no threat. "See? You have nothing to fear."

"How long have you been standing there?"

"A while."

"Where are my friends?"

"I have no idea."

Blade took a stride and aimed at the smaller man's forehead. "Tell me the truth."

"Or what? You'll shoot me? I think not." Morlock chuckled. "You won't kill a defenseless man, boy."

"Don't tempt me."

Morlock nodded at the stairs. "I saw your fight. If you were a born killer, you would have pulled your knives instead of trying to best Elphinstone with your hands and feet." He paused. "My compliments, by the way. No one has ever beaten him before."

"Where is he now?"

"How would I know? Probably nursing his wounds."

"And where's your wife?"

"My darling Endora is taking her nightly stroll."

Blade lowered his rifle barrel a few inches. Now that he had Morlock right where he wanted him, he didn't know what to do. By all rights he should put an end to the man's reign of terror by terminating him on the spot, but he couldn't bring himself to fire. Morlock was right, damn him. Blade wasn't a cold-blooded killer. "We need to talk," he said lamely.

"Indeed we do. That's why I'm here. I knew you entered the underground through the portal in the mausoleum and came down to meet you."

"How did you know?"

Morlock grinned. "That's my little secret." He shifted and gestured upward. "Must we stand here in the draft to discuss what's on your mind? Why not come upstairs with me where we can have our chat in a civilized fashion?"

"Lead the way," Blade said, keeping the Marlin trained on the thin man's back as Morlock led the way toward ground level. His every instinct told him not to let down his guard for an instant. For the time being, though, he had to play along, at least until he knew the fate of Hickok and Geronimo. 'Where's Grell?" he asked.

"You know about him, do you?"

"Just answer the question."

"Very well. I'd imagine he's out trying to round up the serfs. Eventually they'll stop playing their games and let themselves be herded together."

"Just like cattle," Blade stated bitterly.

"In a way, they are."

"Where did they come from? What have you done to them?"

"I'll explain everything once we're comfortable."

Blade fell silent until they reached the ground floor. The sight of candles flickering in holders at regular intervals along the corridor prompted an observation. "I thought all of you can see in the dark."

"Our night vision is exceptional, but we're not completely weaned from a dependence on light. We usually keep a few candles lit after dark," Morlock said and began to climb the next flight.

"Where are you going?"

"The chamber I have in mind is on the third floor."

"What's wrong with one on this floor?"

Morlock paused to look down. "Not a thing, but the sitting room I have in mind is very comfortable and private. We won't be disturbed there."

Who would disturb them? Blade wondered, reluctantly following all the way to the third landing. He stayed on the small man's heels as they went right to the second door, which was wide open. Inside was a lavishly furnished room. Instead of candles, a kerosene lantern provided moderate illumination. "You must have a kerosene storage tank somewhere," he commented, crossing to a wooden chair.

"Take that one, why don't you?" Morlock suggested, pointing at an easy chair near the sofa.

Since it made no difference to the youth, he sat where Morlock wanted.

"And yes, we do have an underground storage tank," the master of the castle disclosed enroute to the sofa. "It's almost dry after all these years, so we conserve what little usable kerosene we have left. When I knew you were coming, I lit a lantern in preparation."

"How did you, by the way?"

"I'll get to that in a bit," Morlock said, taking a seat and folding his left leg over his right. "Would you care for refreshments?"

"Just information," Blade said, not knowing what to make of his host's continued civility. It must be a trick of some kind. At the first hint of hostility, he'd put a bullet in the bastard's brain. He was safe as long as he had the rifle and his Bowies.

"Very well. Where would you like me to begin? With the serfs?"

"That would be nice."

"I overheard enough to know you believe the darling creatures are little better than slaves. Am I right?"

"They *are* slaves."

"Correct me if I'm wrong, but I believe the definition of a slave is someone completely under the domination of another person, someone who is the property of another. Would you agree?"

"Sounds accurate enough to me."

"Then your accusation is unfounded. You heard Tabitha and Selwyn. Do they consider themselves slaves? Absolutely not. They like the life they live and have no desire to change. They're happy," Morlock said. "Would you begrudge them such a blessing?"

Blade disregarded the disquieting question and tried another tack. "Where did they come from?"

"The serfs have served the Morlock clan since shortly after the war—"

"Wait a minute," Blade interrupted. "Is Morlock your first or last name?"

"Morlock is the family name. Moray Morlock was the first lord of Castle Orm."

"Then what's your first name?"

"Angus," Morlock replied, smirking.

Why did he do that? Blade asked himself. "Okay. Back to the serfs. Who were their ancestors? Where did they come from?"

"As I understand it, a dozen survivors showed up here about a week after the missiles were launched. They were suffering from radiation sickness. Moray took them in and let them live in the lower levels. Eventually most of them recovered, and they decided to stay here and work for Moray in exchange for their lodging."

"So the current serfs are their descendants?"

"Aye. Over the years their skin has become paler and paler, and now they're strictly nocturnal."

The explanation was plausible, but Blade felt he was being deceived. He couldn't put a finger on the reason. Perhaps it was Morlock's smug expression and superior air. "And where did Grell come from?"

"Moray found him in the woods ten years after the war."

Blade sat up. "Impossible. That would make Grell close to ninety years-old."

"He is. The serfs even refer to him as the immortal one since three generations of them have known and feared him. Grell was just a pup when Moray stumbled on him hiding in a thicket. Moray liked the wee creature and gave it a home. Ever since Grell has been the Morlock watchdog."

"What kind of mutation is he?"

"I don't know. Moray believed a bear embryo underwent a radiation-induced transformation. If you've seen Grell, you know that no bear grows to such a massive size." Morlock shrugged. "Who knows what his parents were?"

Blade thoughtfully pursed his lips, debating whether to pry into another disturbing matter, and decided to try an oblique approach. "Did Moray ever marry?"

"Yes."

"Another survivor?"

"Aye. Bands of wanderers would travel through the area from time to time. His wife, Constance, was a refugee from the Twin Cities."

And what about your wife? Blade wanted to inquire, but couldn't bring himself to.

"Are you certain I can't entice you to take some refreshment? I took the liberty of having a tray of food set out in the next room."

"I'm not hungry.'"

"Too bad. We have excellent wine and cheese."

Wine? Blade wondered if enough of it might loosen Morlock's lips. Perhaps a glass or two of wine was in order. He'd do anything to uncover a clue concerning his friends. "All right. Some wine can't hurt."

Again Morlock smirked and stood. He walked toward a closed door in the east wall. "Follow me. You can select whatever you want."

Blade held the rifle down low as he crossed to the doorway. His host went through first, and he took three strides himself before he realized he'd been suckered.

Displaying unexpected speed, Morlock darted to the left and grabbed a lever on the wall.

Taken unawares, Blade was sluggish in reacting. "Don't touch that!" he warned and began to bring the barrel up. Too late.

Morlock yanked on the lever.

Blade's finger was tightening on the trigger when the floor fell out from beneath his feet.

CHAPTER FIFTEEN

Gruesome visions of a pit lined with sharp stakes at the bottom filled Blade's mind as he plummeted straight down, enveloped by darkness, his arms above his head, the useless rifle clutched in his left hand. It took a few seconds for him to realize he was hurtling down a metal shaft toward an uncertain fate.

Damn his stupidity!

Anger supplanted the initial shock, anger at his gullibility. He'd waltzed right into the trap with both eyes open. Attila or any of the other experienced Warriors would never have let themselves be so blatantly duped. Being a novice was no excuse. Even novices were expected to exercise basic common sense.

The shaft angled to the right, then the left, in gradual curves designed to retard the speed of passage.

Blade's elbows and knees banged and scraped on the sides, and when he lifted his head and tried to see the bottom his forehead struck the top with a resounding crack. The descent went so long that he estimated the shaft must drop down into the underground levels. When he began to wonder if it would ever end, it did.

Shooting out of the mouth like a tongue out of a lizard, Blade plummeted over ten feet into an enormous tank of stagnant water. He hit with a loud splash and went under, instinctively holding his breath but unable to prevent the warm liquid from filling his nose and ears. A bitter taste filled his mouth, almost gagging him, and then his boots hit bottom and he shoved off, kicking desperately for the top.

He burst from the surface and inhaled deeply, grateful merely to be alive. Shaking his head and wiping his arm across his face, he blinked and looked about him, treading water to stay afloat. To his consternation he found himself imprisoned, enclosed on all four sides by clear glass or plastic walls rising over ten feet above the water.

It was like a gigantic fish tank.

Blade swam to one side and took stock. The depth was 12 feet. The length and width were the same, ten feet both ways. He reached out and touched the wall, deciding the substance must be a hard plastic. Never in a million years would he be able to climb so smooth a surface. And since he couldn't get a purchase for his legs either, he was ingeniously snared and effectively helpless.

The water had a brownish tinge and gave off a foul odor.

Abruptly realizing there must be a light source nearby, Blade surveyed the chamber in which the tank was located. It dwarfed all the others. Fifty feet high and seventy in length, the walls were composed of large, square stones, and the ceiling of immense wooden beams. More thick candles mounted on the walls provided marginal illumination. Far off on the right, at the top of a flight of wooden stairs, stood a broad wooden door.

He swung to the left and received a pleasant shock. Aligned against the wall were five metal cages, the bars on each spaced six inches apart, and two were occupied by unconscious figures.

Hickok and Geronimo!

Elated, Blade swam to the left side of the tank and stared happily at his companions until a horrifying thought occurred to him. What if they were dead? He licked his lips and called out. "Hey! Sleepyheads! Rise and shine!"

There was no reaction.

Intensely worried, Blade yelled louder. "Wake up, you dummies! It's me, Blade."

At last Geronimo stirred, groaning and rolling onto his back. His arms moved feebly.

"Geronimo, wake up!"

The insistent shout had an effect. Geronimo's eyelids fluttered, and after a few seconds he opened his eyes and sat up, gazing in confusion at his surroundings until his gaze alighted on the tank. Recognition brought a flood of awareness, and he suddenly rose to his knees. "Blade! What's going on?" He seized one of the bars. "Where in the world are we?"

"In an underground chamber below Castle Orm," Blade called out. His legs were beginning to tire and he wished he could rest for a while, but there was no place in the tank to gain a firm footing. "What happened to you? How did they catch you?"

Geronimo rubbed the back of his head and stood. "I'm not sure. The last thing I remember is running around the corner and not seeing any sign of Hickok or the serfs. I stopped and was turning when something or someone rose out of the shadows at the base of the wall and clobbered me but good." He paused. "I think it was Elphinstone."

"Morlock captured me," Blade revealed, without bothering to elaborate.

"Have you seen Hik—" Geronimo began and looked to his left. Beaming, he stepped to the side of his cage. "Nathan! On your feet, you goof."

The gunfighter didn't budge.

Geronimo reached through the bars and tried to grab Hickok's cage, but it was inches out of reach. He desisted and cupped his hands to his mouth. "Yo, Nathan! I know you need your beauty sleep, but don't go overboard."

Hickok finally moved his arms. His head bobbed, he licked his lips, and his eyes snapped open. "Where am I?" he bellowed, sitting up. "Where's the lowlife who hit me?" He saw the tank, did a double take and glanced in both directions. Discovering Geronimo, he did another double take, then chuckled.

"What can you possibly find amusing?" the Blackfoot inquired.

"Since you two clowns are here, it's a safe bet I'm not in heaven."

"You're still on Earth, dimwit. Under Morlock's castle."

The gunfighter shoved up, his hands falling to his holster—his empty holsters. "Hey! Where are my six-shooters?"

It was Blade who found them. He noticed a table at the end of the row of cages and distinguished a small pile of weapons. "Over there," he shouted, pointing.

Hickok looked and fumed. "Some hombre is going to pay for takin' my Colts. Nobody takes my guns—ever!"

"How did they manage to catch you?" Blade yelled so his voice would carry over the top of the tank.

"I was after those fairies, as I recollect. I ran into the yard, thinkin' I was about to catch 'em, but they were all gone. I didn't know if they went on around the blamed castle or lit into the trees, and then I saw one of those fancy tombs was open. So I just kept on going, right inside, and I was about to give a call and let you know where I was when the door swung shut and someone bashed me on the head," the gunfighter explained.

"Probably Elphinstone," Blade said. "He's been a busy bee tonight."

"Wait'll I get my revolvers back," Hickok snapped. "I'll teach that yahoo a lesson."

"How are we going to get out of this mess?" Geronimo asked.

Blade wanted an answer to that one himself. After all he'd been through, after the strain of the chase and the fight, his limbs were already weary. The sustained effort of staying above the surface only aggravated his condition. He found it hard to keep his grip on the Marlin.

"Are you holdin' your rifle, pard?" Hickok inquired in amazement.

"Yeah. Why?"

"Try to shoot your way out of that overgrown goldfish bowl. A couple of shots should crack one of those walls, easy."

"What if they're bulletproof?"

"Then the ricochet might hit you," Hickok said. "But what does a little scratch matter if it gets us out of this dungeon?"

Blade tapped the nearest wall with the Marlin, debating the merits of the gunfighter's suggestion. He still had no idea whether the substance was glass or plastic, but a few rounds might just do the trick. There wasn't enough water to do more than cover the floor to a depth of two or three inches, at most, so none of them need worry about drowning. His main concern was the wall. Would it break cleanly or with jagged edges? If the latter, he might be cut badly when the water poured from the tank. "I don't know," he said uncertainly.

"What's wrong with the idea?"

"I could be killed."

"Don't sweat the small stuff, pard. It'll be a piece of cake."

Geronimo snickered. "Easy for you to say, Nathan. You're not doing the slicing."

"And what the blazes is that crack supposed to mean?"

Their discussion was interrupted by the opening of the big wooden door. In strolled the master of Castle Orm bearing a five-gallon bottle in his hand. The bottle contained a brownish liquid.

"Ahhh, good. I see all of you are awake."

Hickok grabbed hold of two bars and shook them violently. "Let us out of here, you vermin!"

"Sticks and stones, boy," Morlock said chuckling as he walked toward them. "Are all of you comfortable?"

"Up yours," Hickok declared.

"What he said," Geronimo added.

Morlock glanced at the giant. "Enjoying your swim?" he asked scornfully and cackled.

"The guy is off his rocker," Hickok commented.

"Must be related to you," Geronimo stated.

Blade pressed his right hand to the wall, treading water with an effort, wishing he could throttle Angus Morlock's skinny neck. "What do you plan to do with us?" he snapped.

"It should be obvious, even to childish morons like yourselves."

"Give me my shootin' irons and I'll show you who's childish," Hickok declared.

Walking up to the tank, Morlock halted and grinned at Blade. "To answer your question, I plan to dispose of the three of you."

"Why?"

"Need you ask?" Morlock snorted. "Did you really think I would allow you to leave the Domain so that you could return to Humboldt and tell others all about us?"

"But you threw us out this morning."

"And you were watched every minute after that until night fell. Had you left the valley, I would have sent Grell and Elphinstone after you tonight. One way or the other, you'd never have reached Humboldt alive."

"Shows how much you know," Hickok said. "We're

not from Humboldt, yo-yo."

Morlock took the news in stride. "It doesn't really matter where you are from. By morning, all three of you will be dead."

Blade glanced at the top of the tank, then scrutinized the water. How did Morlock intend to kill him? Simply let him tire out and sink to the bottom?

"If you kill us, you'll be sorry," Hickok said.

"I won't regret my actions in the least," Morlock replied. "You're interlopers who threaten the peace and security of the Domain. I have an obligation to my family and the serfs to protect them at all costs." He deposited the bottle at his feet.

"Who are you trying to kid?" Blade said. "You have an obligation to protect yourself. You're afraid a group of survivors will learn what's been going on here and put a stop to it."

"To what? My alleged mistreatment of the serfs? We've already discussed that issue, and you know they're quite content."

"I'm not talking about your slaves. I'm referring to what you've done to everyone who has passed by your castle." Blade indicated the chamber with a sweep of his head. "This torture chamber must see a lot of business."

The diminutive man laughed. "This is my holding room. The torture chamber is in the next room on the right."

"How many innocent people have you killed over the years?"

"Those I've slain deserved to die," Morlork said. "And I don't keep a tally. Perhaps there have been three dozen."

The number appalled Blade. "Did you build this tank yourself?"

"Heavens, no. Great-grandfather Moray had this room built. From the information in his diary, he used the facilities much more than I do."

"So Moray started the tradition of slaying all outsiders?"

"Aye. He knew outsiders would never be able to appreciate our way of life."

"And Moray was responsible for having the secret passages constructed?"

"Aye."

"And those survivors you told me about, the ones who became the serfs, he didn't take them in out of the goodness of his heart. He probably forced them down here at gunpoint and imprisoned them, then tortured them until they were mental vegetables."

Morlock laughed. "You're not as dumb as you look, boy."

"I also know about your family tree."

Sudden anger tinged Morlock's cheeks crimson. "Yes, you definitely are a bright one. Not that the information can have any significance to you."

"You're sick."

"Who the hell are you to judge me, boy? What do you know about life? Our way was established centuries ago. The Morlock clan has always been close-knit."

"In more ways than one."

A malevolent sneer curled Morlock's mouth. "I'll enjoy killing you." He clasped his hands behind his back and walked close to the cages. "Please be patient. After your friend is finished, you'll each have your turns."

"You're making a major mistake," Geronimo said. "We have other friends who know where we were headed. They'll send a search party."

"Let them. By then I'll have the crack in the outer wall repaired, and they'll have no way to get inside. They'll learn nothing and leave empty-handed."

"Have it all figured out, huh?" Hickok remarked.

"I'm a Morlock. The males in our family have always enjoyed an extremely high I.Q."

"Does that include Elphinstone?" Blade interjected.

Angus shrugged. "There are exceptions to every rule.. He's an inferior idiot, useless for breeding purposes. I, on the other hand, am a genius."

"You're a madman," Blade corrected him.

Morlock returned to the side of the tank and smiled up at the youth. "Enough idle chatter. Are you ready to die?"

CHAPTER SIXTEEN

Blade watched Angus Morlock pick up the five-gallon bottle and walk around to the opposite side of the tank where the murky water concealed him from view. He glanced at his friends, neither of whom could see Morlock either, and started to dog-paddle across the tank. A metallic scraping noise caused him to stop, and a moment later he saw the upper end of a ladder being placed against the tank wall. The top rung came within inches of the upper edge.

"Be careful, Blade," Geronimo yelled.

"Use the rifle," Hickok urged.

The ladder bounced slightly as Morlock climbed above the water level and beamed at the giant. Secure under his left arm was the bottle. "Did you miss me?" he asked and tittered.

Blade arched his spine, letting his upper back float to relieve some of the strain on his tired legs. He hefted the Marlin, his eyes on Morlock.

"I wouldn't waste my time using the rifle, if I were you. This plastic in shatterproof. You could smash it with a sledgehammer, and it wouldn't crack.''

''Has anyone ever tried?''

The question elicited another cackle. Morlock climbed laboriously to the top of the ladder, pausing every three or four rungs to adjust his grip on the bottle.

What was in there? Blade wondered. What was worth such effort? He glimpsed small, dark forms being swished about but couldn't identify them. Goose bumps broke out all over his skin.

Morlock was careful not to expose himself. He kept his head below the plastic rim and grinned. ''You must be curious about my surprise package.''

Blade wasn't about to give him the courtesy of a response.

''There is a stream about a quarter of a mile south of the castle. Quite by accident I discovered that a marvelous mutation inhabits its water. I went fishing one day, tossed in my line and pulled out one of these amazing creatures.''

Lightly stroking the Marlin's trigger, Blade waited for the madman to lift the bottle above the rim.

''I had no idea what I'd caught and foolishly tried to remove it from my hook. The thing clamped onto me and wouldn't let go. I was forced to return to the castle and used a candle to burn it off. By then, of course, I'd lost a pint or two of blood.''

Geronimo and Hickok were listening attentively, their countenances reflecting their worry.

Morlock grunted and tightened his hold on the bottle. ''My research indicates this particular form of mutation once existed as common flatworms. As you might know, free-living flatworms exist in ponds, streams and oceans all over the world.''

Blade's forehead knit in perplexity. Worms? The man had worms in there? What possible threat could worms pose?

''Some flatworms closely resemble leeches, which might explain these mutations. Of course, few grow as large or become aggressive, but radiation is notorious for drastically altering genetic traits," Morlock said, starting to raise the bottle toward the rim.

Blade held the rifle at water level, his stomach muscles tightening. The madman must not be accustomed to having victims fight back, he reasoned, or else Morlock wouldn't make such blatant mistakes.

The demented lord looked into the bottle and snickered. "Are you thirsty, my little ones?" He glanced at the giant. "They haven't been fed in days. I'd imagine they're famished."

A few more inches, Blade thought, his visage impassive.

"Time for the festivities," Morlock said and hoisted the container above the edge of the plastic wall. He held it steady in preparation for upending the contents into the tank.

Blade was ready. He snapped the Marlin to his shoulders, took a hasty bead on the middle of the bottle and fired. The booming of the 45-70 almost deafened him.

The slug smashed the bottle to pieces and sent a shower of glass, water and mutations spraying down on both sides of the wall. Most of it struck a shocked Morlock full in the face, and screaming, he brought up his hands to shield his eyes and lost his balance. Desperately he tried to grab a rung, but he plummeted from the ladder.

All this Blade barely noticed. He had problems of his own. Three dark forms had dropped into the tank and disappeared in the soup. He swam to the far corner and pressed his back to the wall, waiting for whatever they were to attack.

They didn't waste any time.

Something crested the surface and made a beeline for the youth, its slender shape visible as a dark brown blur, throwing off a narrow wake.

Blade levered a fresh round into the chamber, pressed the rifle to his shoulder and tried to track the speeding mutation. He squeezed off a shot when the thing was only inches from the end of the barrel, and the mutation promptly dived. He had no idea whether he'd scored or not.

"What are they?" Geronimo called out.

"Use the rife on the wall! Use the rifle on the wall!" Hickok stressed urgently.

Feeding in another round, Blade turned right and left, his legs kicking vigorously. He envisioned one of them going for his groin and involuntarily shuddered.

Suddenly Morlock appeared, his features a mask of fury, blood seeping from a half-dozen cuts on his face and neck. Dangling from his left cheek and his forehead were two of the mutations. He shook his right fist at the giant and bellowed, "Damn you! Damn you all to hell!"

Blade couldn't help but look.

The mutations were a foot in length and two inches in width, except at the center where they tapered to an inch. Their bodies were essentially flat, but their heads were round and the size of a grown man's fist. Somehow the creatures had latched onto Morlock and were sucking his blood.

"I'll be back!" the madman shrieked and ran toward the door, tugging in vain on his unwanted appendages.

Blade gulped and scanned the water. Where were they? Had the shot deterred them? Even more important, how could he get out of there before the things tried again?

He stiffened when he felt a nudge on his right ankle. It had to be one of the mutations! The nudge was repeated on his shin, then his knee and his inner thigh. The thing was working its way up his body, perhaps seeking naked flesh.

Blade stared straight down, transferred the rifle to his left hand and drew his right Bowie. He distinguished the rippling form of the bloodsucker several inches below his belt, writhing snakelike. Elevating the knife above his head, he froze until the thing was level with his belt, then speared the point into the water.

The Bowie connected, slicing the creature open, and black fluid poured from the wound. Instantly the thing angled toward the bottom and vanished.

Two down, or at least wounded, Blade congratulated himself. But he'd been lucky. He couldn't expect to hold them off forever. Had Morlock succeeded in dumping in the entire bottle, he'd probably have a dozen of the mutations gorging on his blood. He glanced up at the transparent walls, racking his brain for a way out. They were shatterproof, Morlock had boasted. A sledgehammer wouldn't crack them, which meant his Bowies were useless.

Another thin shape materialized on the surface eight feet away and swam toward the youth as if propelled by a rocket.

Blade saw it coming and braced to meet the slender monster, swinging his right arm on high and bringing the Bowie down again at just the right moment, trying to cleave the creature in two. He missed.

He glimpsed a circular head rearing out of the water, a head consisting entirely of a gaping mouth ringed by tiny, tapered teeth. From the mouth protruded a tubular tongue six inches long. And then the mutation smacked into his abdomen next to his navel, and an incredible pain lanced his gut. Those tiny teeth sank in and held fast. He doubled over, feeling as if someone was gouging his midriff with a scorching poker.

It was the thing's tongue!

Blade realized the creature was seeking a vein or an artery. With a supreme effort he straightened, stuck the knife in his mouth with the sharp edge outward and tried to seize the writhing horror. Its slippery body squished through his fingers again and again. In desperation he seized it near the head and finally succeeded in getting a firm grip. He yanked, but the mutation was locked onto his body.

"Use the rifle on the wall!" Hickok bellowed. "Use the rifle on the wall!"

In the back of his mind Blade wished the dummy would shut up. If a sledgehammer wouldn't do the job, what good would his rifle do? He wrenched on the flatworm, his right arm bulging, and his hands slipped off. There was no way he could remove it unless he got a firm footing. Which brought him back to square one.

He spied another of the creatures swimming slowly on the other side of the tank.

Dear Spirit, what should he do? He pounded the plastic in frustration, and then inspiration struck. Sure, a sledgehammer wouldn't work, but a sledge delivered its force over a broader area than a bullet. A 45-70 was one of the most powerful rifles ever made. Its thick, blunt bullet could plow through thick brush to bag a deer or an elk. At point-blank range, what would the effect be on the plastic?

There was only one way to find out.

Twisting, Blade jammed the barrel against the glass several inches below the water line. If he was wrong, the ricochet might well kill him. But it was either that or let the mutations slowly suck him lifeless.

He fired.

The shot was muffled by the water. His arms were driven backwards by the recoil.

Blade leaned closer and saw a dent in the plastic. The bullet hadn't penetrated. He guessed the slug had flattened and sank to the bottom. But the dent was encouraging. The creature's tongue fluttered around inside his stomach, adding incentive to his limbs as he worked the lever. He placed the barrel directly on the dent and squeezed the trigger.

The 45-70 did its job. The high-powered round drilled through the plastic, trailed by a stream of water that splashed onto the floor below.

One hole wouldn't suffice. Blade levered the fourth

round home, then groped in his back pocket and extracted three more shells. He quickly loaded and pressed the rifle to the wall again, only this time three inches below the hole. Once more he fired, expecting to dent the plastic.

This time the first shot bored through, producing a second stream, but it did something more. The concentration of pressure at the two holes as the water gushed out put an immense strain on the plastic between and surrounding the holes, and the pressure accomplished what the Marlin alone never could.

A resounding snap sounded, and suddenly a network of fine lines mushroomed in the wall. The next moment those lines became cracks, the water hissing and cascading from the tank.

Blade tried to paddle away from the wall, but he was too late. The whole section buckled and split, and an irresistible wave carried him through the gaping opening onto the chamber floor. He fell to his knees, nearly losing his grip on the rifle, and was buffeted by the escaping water. The reeking liquid enveloped his momentarily, then dispersed across the chamber.

"Blade!" Geronimo shouted.

His stomach on fire, Blade slowly stood and staggered toward the cages. The water was up to his ankles, and he had to be careful not to slip. He halted and stared at the repulsive thing hanging from his abdomen. Grimacing, he wrapped his right hand around it, squeezed with all of his might and wrenched savagely.

The upper edge of the mutation's mouth peeled off, but it still hung on.

Blade grit his teeth, closed his eyes and pulled like he had never pulled on anything before. For half a minute nothing happened, then abruptly the creature popped loose, its blood-covered tongue sliding out and flopping in the air. In a frenzy of rage, he repeatedly smashed the rifle stock on the thing until its body and tongue both hung limp. Disgusted by the violation of his body and still not satisfied the mutation was dead, he placed the flatworm under his boot and ground it into the stone until a sarcastic voice made him realize what he was doing.

"I think the sucker is a goner, pard."

Blade stopped grinding his heel and looked at his friends. "I guess you're right," he said softly.

"Why don't you find a way to get us out?" Hickok suggested. "And hurry it up before the runt and his ugly pals show up."

The reminder sparked Blade to action. He hurried to the cages and searched the nearby wall and the table for keys. There were none.

"You might need to get the keys from Morlock," Geronimo said.

"No," Blade responded.

"Then how do you figure to get us out?" Hickok asked.

Before Blade could answer, Geronimo extended his right arm between the bars and pointed. "Look!"

Turning, Blade beheld a sight that chilled his blood.

Most of the floor was now covered with water, and swimming about in search of prey were a dozen or so mutations, going every which way, their slim forms easy to spot.

"We don't have to worry about them," Blade declared. "They can't suck blood unless they touch flesh, and all of us have on footwear.

"But what if they can crawl as well as swim?" Geronimo remarked. "They could come right up our legs."

The idea intensified Blade's nausea. "Take this," he said, handing the rifle to Hickok.

"What are you fixin' to do?"

"Watch." Blade planted both feet firmly in front of the door and gripped the bar, one hand above the lock, the other below it. He winked at the gunfighter, inhaled and applied all of his prodigious strength to forcing the door open. His muscles rippled and contorted, his neck swelling and the veins expanding. Breathing in short, loud spurts, he battled the metal bar for a minute. Two. Then slowly, creaking noisily, the bar began to bend. Next the lock tilted outward. At last, with the sweat pouring down Blade's face and his chest aching terribly, the lock gave way with a grinding retort.

"Took you long enough," Hickok muttered, stepping out and surveying the chamber. "You work at freeing Geronimo, and I'll keep you covered."

Despite being weary to his core, Blade moved to the next cage and repeated the procedure. This door resisted longer, draining his flagging energy, and just when he thought he couldn't do it, the lock snapped, making him stumble backward. He caught himself and swayed.

"Are you sure you're all right?" Geronimo asked, emerging.

"Fine," Blade said. "Just give me a chance to catch my breath."

"We don't have much time, pard," Hickok mentioned and returned the Marlin. He ran to the table, picked up his cherished Colts and grinned. "Let's get to kickin' butt."

Geronimo went over to retrieve his weapons. "What's our first move?" he asked.

"We'll search this castle from top to bottom," Blade said, arching his back to relieve a cramp.

"And when we find the runt?" Hickok inquired, walking back. He twirled the Colts into their holsters.

"The Morlock rein of terror ends today," Blade vowed, glancing over his shoulder to check on the mutations. His eyes widened at the sight of five of the grotesque genetic deviations converging on him from all directions.

CHAPTER SEVENTEEN

Blade raised the rifle and aimed at the nearest creature, feeling sick again at the thought of one of those things inserting its tongue into his body. Try as he might, he couldn't seem to hold the barrel steady.

"Let me," Hickok stated, stepping past the giant, a grin curling his lips. "Eat these, bloodsuckers," he said and drew both Colts in a blur of ambidextrous speed. Five shots boomed in succession.

Blade was astonished by his friend's accuracy. With each shot a mutation flipped into the air or skidded backwards, its thin form neatly punctured, then thrashed wildly in its death throes, spraying water right and left.

"Let's skedaddle, pard," the gunfighter proposed. He began reloading the spent rounds, his gaze constantly roving over the floor.

No urging was necessary. Blade hurried to the wooden stairs and climbed them to the door. Surprisingly, Morlock hadn't bothered to lock it, but with those vile creatures sucking blood from his face, he'd probably been too preoccupied to give thought to the door.

"Let's clear up one detail before we step out there," Hickok said as Blade pulled the door open. "Do we shoot to kill on sight?"

There was no hesitation on Blade's part. "Yes."

Hickok chuckled. "Maybe you'll make a decent Warrior after all."

They entered a dark corridor. From somewhere came a fluttering sound, like the beating of bat wings.

Blade took the lead and advanced for dozens of yards before he noticed an unlit candle in a holder to his left. "Wait a second," he said and felt in his pockets for the boxes of matches. All three were soaked on the outside. Doubting he would find a match that wasn't drenched, he opened the boxes and felt for a dry one.

"Where'd you find those?" Hickok asked.

"In a storage room."

"Did you happen to see any dynamite?"

"No."

"Shucks."

At the center of one of the boxes Blade found five dry matches. He quickly lit one, removed the candle from the holder and applied the flame to the wick. "Geronimo, will you gather up the matches?" he requested. "If we dry them out, we might be able to use them."

"Sure." The Blackfoot squatted and put the boxes in his pockets. The four dry matches went in a separate one.

Blade resumed walking, holding the candle aloft to give them a ten-foot radius of dim illumination. He tried not to think of what would happen should they encounter Grell, but an image of the fiery eyed beast haunted his every step.

The corridor connected to the central stairs, where a whispering draft almost extinguished the flickering flame. Blade cupped the same hand holding the rifle around the top of the candle and started upward into the wicked heart of the festering evil.

At the next level they paused. There were four forks

extending on a line with the four main points of a compass. From the southern branch light laughter arose.

"Serfs, you reckon?" Hickok commented.

A few moments later six pale figures materialized and pranced gaily toward the three youths.

Blade smiled, relieved to encounter some of the innocents first. They drew close and halted, giggling childishly. Tabitha and Selwyn weren't among them. "Hello," he said in greeting.

"Hello, sir," one of the males responded.

"What are you doing?" Blade asked casually.

"We're waiting for the great mast to come back so we can play pincushion."

Only then did Blade see the knives in their hands. Shocked, he lowered his arm. "Pincushion?"

"Yes, sir." The male tittered. "Sometimes Master Morlock puts outers in a cage. We get to surround the cage, and when he opens the door we play pincushion with our knives."

Horrified, Blade glanced at his companions, then at the presumed innocents. "Do all of the serfs play pincushion?"

"Yes, sir. The masts gather all of us together for the treat. Master Morlock gave us these knives an hour ago and told us to wait on this level until the rest of the serfs come back. Then the fun will begin."

"How can you describe stabbing a human being to death as fun?"

"Oh, it's terrific," the male stated, and several of the others laughed. "The outers always scream and beg and whine while we poke them with our knives. Some of them put up a wonderful fight. In the end, though, they always fall down and go to sleep."

"Why don't you put those knives down and go play something else?" Blade suggested.

One of the women answered. "We can't do that, sir. The great mast gave us orders, and we must obey."

Blade stiffened when a harsh voice bellowed down from one of the upper levels.

"Felcram, do you hear me?"

"Yes, Master Morlock," the male answered, gazing all around as if he couldn't figure out where the voice came from.

"Kill the three outers!"

"These three?"

"Yes. Kill them now."

"Now, wait a minute—" Blade began, thinking he could persuade the serfs to let them pass in peace. Suddenly the six attacked, cackling with glee and swinging their knives maniacally. He swung the Marlin to keep a man and a woman at bay while holding the candle aloft.

Geronimo used the rifle in a similar fashion, fending off two males, blocking repeated swings. "I don't want to harm you," he said. "Please stop."

They only chortled.

Lacking a rifle, Hickok was twisting and dodging to evade a pair of women intent on burying their knives in his chest. "We don't have time for this," he said, blocking a fierce swing with his forearm, then slugging the woman in the jaw. She collapsed at his feet.

"Please stop," Blade pleaded. "You don't know what you're doing."

"Sure we do," one of the males said. "We're playing pincushion."

Blade knew the three of them wouldn't be able to evade the knives forever. There had to be a way to drive the serfs off without hurting them. As he side-stepped a lunge at his legs, he inadvertently lowered the candle and saw both males hastily back up, their eyes narrowed. He remembered how Tabitha and Selwyn had dreaded going near the campfire and grinned. Instead of using his rifle, he now swung the candle from side to side, keeping it at eye level, careful not to let the flame go out, and moved towards the serfs.

Both males shielded their eyes, whined and fled.

As if on an unseen cue, the rest of the band joined their fellows in flight except for the woman Hickok had decked.

"Good riddance," the gunfighter stated.

"Why did they run?" Geronimo asked.

"They can't stand bright light," Blade said. "Even a candle shoved in their faces is more than they can take."

"Too bad we don't have another torch," Hickok said.

Blade watched the retreating serfs until they took a left and disappeared. He gazed up the stairs and snapped. "Let's go."

They ascended quickly, alert for traps or an ambush, until once more they stood on the ground floor. The candles along the corridor caused intermittent shadows to dance and writhe like ethereal, inky demons.

A strident howl of glee echoed to their ears from above.

"It's Morlock," Hickok fumed.

In verification came a taunting shout. "Did you like playing with my serfs, boys?"

"Show yourself!" Blade yelled.

"And spoil all the glorious entertainment yet to come? You must be joking."

"You can't hide from us forever," Blade called up.

"I don't intend to, dear boy. You'll see me when you least expect it." Morlock paused. "It's so rare for us to have guests such as yourselves. This is a very special night, and we want to prolong the amusement for as long as we can."

"I can't wait to plug that cowchip," Hickok muttered.

"Never happen, boy," Morlock said.

None of the youths replied, and silence gripped the castle.

Geronimo was the first to speak. "How did he do that?"

"Do what, pard?" the gunfighter asked.

"How did he hear your last remark? He must be three floors above us, at least."

Blade mulled the same question. Earlier, Morlock had

claimed to know the moment he entered the underground through the mausoleum. How? Had Morlock watched him from a hidden passage? But a secret passageway wouldn't explain overhearing a hushed remark from three floors up.

"Maybe we should split up," Hickok proposed. "We can each take a floor and get this over with a lot sooner than if we stick together."

"No," Blade said. "We'll do this as a team, as if we were a Warrior triad."

"But Geronimo isn't a Warrior yet."

"Keep rubbing it in, why don't you?" Geronimo cracked.

"We'll start with the second floor," Blade suggested and went cautiously up to the next landing. There wasn't a candle lit along its entire length, so he raised the one he held and walked to the nearest door. Standing to one side, he nodded.

Geronimo gripped the knob and turned. The door swung inward to reveal typically well-preserved furniture and a thick red carpet.

"Empty," Hickok said.

And so it went. Room after room after room was examined, and in each they discovered furniture and nothing more. They finished with the second floor and moved to the third, where Blade stepped to the second door on the right and threw it open.

The lantern still glowed, but Angus Morlock was nowhere in evidence.

Blade crossed to the door in the east wall, which hung wide, and stared grimly at the square opening and the dangling trapdoor.

"What's this?" Hickok asked.

"Where Morlock pulled a fast one on me."

"I've got news for you, pard. That bozo has been jerkin' us around ever since we got here."

Blade retraced his steps to the hall and continued to search. Three more rooms yielded zilch.

"We're wastin' our time," Hickok complained. "He's likely sittin' behind one of these walls laughin' himself silly at our expense."

"We're not giving up."

The gunfighter snapped his fingers. "Hey, I've got a brainstorm."

"Uh-oh," Geronimo said.

"What's your idea?" Blade asked.

"Let's smoke the rascals out. We'll set fire to the place and wait outside for them to show their faces."

Geronimo pressed a hand to his cheek. "My, why didn't Blade and I think of that?"

"It's brilliant," Hickok bragged.

"Except for one small detail," Geronimo said.

"Like what?"

"The castle is made of *stone.*"

"Oh."

"But you keep thinking, Nathan. It's what you're good at."

"Was that a cut?"

Blade glanced at them. "Will you two clowns clam up?" He shook his head and walked toward a closed door. As far back as he could remember, Hickok and Geronimo had always been at each other's throat in an amiable sort of way. It always amused him that they could verbally rip each other to shreds time and again, but if someone else were to insult either one, then both would be on the offender's case in a flash. Hopefully, once all three of them were Warriors and they were confronted with the full responsibilities of their posts, the nonstop banter would cease. He looked forward to the peace and quiet.

A faint glow rimmed the next door.

Blade motioned for his friends to be ready and tried the knob. Unlike other doors, this one was locked. He stepped back, drew up his right leg and planted his boot next to the knob. The wood held firm.

"Allow me, pard," Hickok said, moving across the

corridor. He lowered his shoulder and ran straight at the door, striking it with a resounding thud that knocked him onto his posterior. The panel shuddered but wasn't even cracked.

Geronimo clucked a few times. "I could have told you that wouldn't work."

"Oh, yeah?" Hickok responded indignantly, rising.

"Yep. You should have used your head."

"How about if I use these?" the gunfighter retorted, and both Colts leaped into his hands. Two shots thundered simultaneously, and the wood above the lock splintered and blew apart. He stepped over and tapped the door with a gun.

Even Blade had to grin when the door swung inward. He entered and halted just over the threshold, astounded by the extraordinary furnishings.

"Wow!" Hickok said. "What is all this?"

"It's a weapons room," Geronimo speculated.

Mounted on every wall and displayed in numerous cases were scores of weapons—swords of every size and type; axes and pikes; dirks, daggers and knives; lances and shields bearing various crests; maces and spiked clubs. Ringing the room at ten foot intervals were complete suits a medieval armor braced by supporting stands. Occupying the middle of the floor were five tables bearing additional ancient arms.

Hickok walked over to the suit of armor and ran his fingers over the polished metal. "Where's Sir Galahad when you need him?"

"I'm impressed, Nathan," Geronimo said, moving to the first table. "I thought your knowledge of history was strictly limited to the Old West."

"I've gone through the same schooling courses you have," Hickok replied. "I'm not ignorant, you know. I remember readin' all about those Knights of the Oval Chamber Pot."

"They were the Knights of the Round Table, nitwit."

"Whatever."

Blade stood to the left of the doorway and admired the collection. Someone, undoubtedly Moray Morlock or one of his ancestors, must have spent a fortune to accumulate such fine, authentic weapons. Perhaps the Morlock clan collected diligently for generations.

The gunfighter knocked on the breastplate and asked, "Is anyone home?"

Geronimo chuckled. "What would you do if it answered?"

"Head for the hills."

"We should keep looking for Morlock," Blade said, motioning at the corridor.

"What's the big rush?" Hickok responded, stepping to the next display of body armor, a huge suit suitable for the Biblical Goliath. "There might be something here we can use."

Blade was about to argue but changed his mind. Technically, he had no authority for bossing the gunfighter around, and he'd rather save his energy for when it was really needed. He absently glanced at the door, at the shattered wood above the lock, then at the source of the light, a lantern resting on a case near the huge suit of armor.

Something about the door and the lantern bothered him, but he couldn't determine the cause. So what if one of the clan left a lantern in the room earlier? So what if the door had been locked? Morlock probably didn't want them to get their hands on any of the weapons.

Geronimo had picked up a weapon resembling a short lance topped by a spike and an odd hatchet. "What were these called?"

"Thingamajigs," Hickok said.

"Thank you, Mr. Middle Ages expert."

"It's a halberd," Blade told them. "They were used in the fifteenth and sixteenth centuries by knights and foot soldiers alike."

"No wonder you always got A's in school," Hickok said. "You have a knack for recallin' all the diddly details that no one else does."

"You remember them," Blade stated. "You just pretend you don't so you can act dumb."

Geronimo looked up. "Why would he want to *act* dumb when it's his natural state?"

"Same to you, turkey," Hickok said. He started to reach toward the visor on the huge armor.

Blade stared at the door again, jarred by an unsettling thought. What if the latern was there because someone had been using it? And what if the door had been locked from the inside, not the outside? He turned to voice his concern to the others.

The gunfighter rapped on the visor and repeated the same question. "Is anyone home?"

From within the armor came a guttural reply that shocked all three youths. "Yes." And with that, the knight attacked.

CHAPTER EIGHTEEN

Hickok was the first to fall. Dumfounded by the development, his lightning reflexes were unable to prevent the knight's right gauntlet from striking him a heavy blow on the left temple. He crumpled with his hands almost to his Colts.

"Nathan!" Geronimo cried and rushed in with the halberd upraised, neglecting to use his rifle in his concern for his friend.

The knight shifted to meet the Blackfoot. When the halberd arched toward his helmet, he blocked the blade with his right vambrace and delivered a left fist to Geronimo's jaw that felled the youth in his tracks.

Leaving only Blade. Too late he'd noticed there was no supporting stand bracing the huge suit. He released the candle and jammed the Marlin to his shoulder. "Don't move!" he warned.

But the knight paid no attention. He clanked to one side and lifted a mace from the wall. Pivoting, his armor creaking loudly, he advanced and elevated the weapon.

"Your armor won't protect you from a bullet," Blade

said and then wondered why he bothered. The person in that suit was an enemy. Hickok and Geronimo were already down. What did it take to get him to do what had to be done?

"Kill," the knight declared gruffly. "Kill."

Blade sighted on the knight's visor and touched the trigger. "Try this on for size," he said and was about to fire when intervention from an unexpected source ruined his aim.

Endora Morlock materialized out of nowhere and batted the barrel upward with her arms just as the Marlin boomed. "No!" she shouted, trying to pull the rifle free.

Angered by her interference, Blade faced her and tried to tug the Marlin from her desperate grip. "Let go," he demanded.

"No," Endora replied passionately. "Don't hurt him."

The scraping of metal joints almost at Blade's left side made him look and jump back, relinquishing his hold on the Marlin to preserve his life. A heartbeat later the mace cleaved the air at the spot where he'd stood.

"Kill," the knight vowed and turned ponderously to keep the youth in the limited field of vision afforded by the slots in the visor.

Blade retreated a yard and assumed an on-guard stance. His Bowies would be useless against armor designed to render its wearer impervious to edged weaponry.

Endora grabbed the knight's elbow. "Leave him alone, Elphinstone!"

"Go away," the brute snapped, jerking his arm loose. "Must kill bad man."

"He's not bad. Please, Elphinstone. Don't fight him."

"Must fight. Father says must kill."

Endora darted around in front of her brother, her face a study of emotional turmoil. "Please," she begged again. "For me, Elphie. For *me.*"

The visor fixed on her earnest visage, and Elphinstone's dull eyes met her beseeching eyes. "For you?"

"Yes. I don't want either of you to be harmed."

"Bad man hurt me."

"But there's no reason to keep on hurting each other."

"Bad man kicked and hit me."

Endora placed her right hand on the breastplate. "We've always been close, Elphie. There's always been just the two of us. You know how much you mean to me. Please don't fight this man any more."

Elphinstone contemplated her appeal in stony silence.

With the rifle held loosely in Endora's left hand, Blade couldn't resist the temptation. He lunged, grasped the barrel and tried to tear it from her hands.

The instant the youth sprang into action, so did Elphinstone. He swung the mace at Blade's arms, forcing the Warrior to skip out of the way empty-handed.

"No!" Endora wailed, but she was rudely shoved aside.

Like a great, mad, lumbering elephant, Elphinstone bore down on Blade, furiously swinging his mace. He clipped Blade's shoulder but failed to connect with a death stroke. Relentlessly he pressed the youth, driving him all the way back to the east wall.

Blade felt the wall bump against his shoulder blades. He looked both ways. Mounted to his left was an axe, and in two strides he had it in his possession.

Undaunted, his brute intellect focused on the sole task of slaying the youth in the leather vest, Elphinstone relentlessly closed in.

Axe met mace in a savage cadence of metallic clanging, a primal pounding of weapon on weapon, the room ringing to their resounding blows.

Blade braced his legs and fought with all the skill at his command. He swung overhand, underhand, from the side and in figure-eight patterns, striving to break through his foe's defenses. Twice he struck Elphinstone's helmet, yet neither blow seemed to have any effect.

Off near the door stood Endora, her left hand covering her mouth, her eyes wide with fear for her brother's life.

Blade's fatigue slowed his movements. He had to fight on two fronts—one with himself, the other with the apish Morlock. Every clash of their weapons jolted his arms to the bone. After a minute of sustained combat he reluctantly gave ground, backing up slowly, on the defensive and not liking it one bit.

On Elphinstone's part, he fought as five men even though encumbered by the weight of the armor. Like a tireless machine he swung and swung and swung, his dull eyes never blinking.

Blade accidentally backed into a standing suit of armor. He stepped to the left, continuing to block a hail of fierce blows, when an idea blossomed that he immediately implemented. Suddenly bounding out of his adversary's reach, he sent the suit of armor crashing to the floor at the brute's feet.

Elphinstone had to tilt his head and stare straight down to avoid tripping over the obstacle, and in that costly moment of distraction he failed to keep his guard up.

Blade whipped the axe in an overhand loop, putting all of his strength and weight into the strike, the blade smashing onto the helmet just above the visor and rocking Elphinstone on his heels. Again Blade struck, this time hitting the helmet on the right side.

The brute staggered.

Both blows had dented the helmet but not pierced the metal. Eager to end the conflict quickly, Blade drew his arms back as far as he could, then drove the axe around and in, slamming it into the visor.

Elphinstone toppled, dropping the mace as he fell and landing on his back with a crash that rattled every weapon and suit of armor in the room.

Stepping closer, Blade lifted the axe on high for the *coup de grace.*

"No!" Endora screamed. "For the love of God, don't!"

Blade hesitated, conscious of the sweat caking his body and his aching muscles and joints. He glanced at her. "Why shouldn't I? He tried to kill me."

"You can't blame him. He doesn't know what he's doing. Haven't you noticed he's feeble-minded?"

Lowering the axe, Blade frowned and moved to his friends. First he checked Geronimo, then Hickok. Both were breathing, simply unconscious, the gunfighter sporting a nasty bruise on his temple.

Endora ran to Elphinstone and pried the visor open with difficulty. She placed her ear to his lips and exclaimed in relief, "You just knocked him out. He'll live."

"And what will happen when he revives?" Blade snapped. "If he comes at me again, I'll be forced to kill him. Which reminds me." He saw the Marlin lying on the carpet and quickly retrieved it, flung the axe aside and levered in a new round.

"If you leave now there won't be more violence," Endora said. "Wake your friends and get out of here."

"We can't leave."

"Can't or won't?"

"Both," Blade said. "We know all about what has been going on here, and we mean to put a stop to it."

Endora's features clouded. "You don't know everything," she said softly. "There are things too horrible to mention."

"Such as the fact your husband is actually your father?"

Stark consternation rippled across Endora's face. She gasped and clutched at her throat. "Who told you?"

"No one."

"Impossible! Someone had to tell you. I'll bet it was one of the serfs. A few of the older ones know our secret," Endora said, her cheeks flushing crimson. Her expression abruptly hardened. "I'll kill every one. I'll have them skinned alive."

"You'll do no such thing," Blade stated. "The Morlock family has caused enough sorrow and comitted too many atrocities as it is."

"Who are you to judge us?"

"Like father, like daughter."

Endora took several steps toward him, her fists clenched in anger. "What the hell is that supposed to mean? And what do you really know about our family history, about the incredible hardships the Morlocks have endured? We were cut off from the rest of the world. To survive we had to resort to incest."

"Don't lie to me," Blade said sternly. "The Morlock clan has practiced incest for centuries."

Astonishment made Endora blink. "How did you know that?"

"I can add two plus two."

"You're smarter than you look. Angus underestimated you from the beginning. He thought he could play with you, have a little fun before he finished off the three of you."

"Where's your father now?"

"I don't know."

Blade made as if to strike her with the rifle. "What did I tell you about lying?"

Recoiling in fear, Endora licked her lips. "Honest. I don't know where he is at this very minute. Probably in the control room."

"The what?"

Realizing she'd given away too much, Endora shook her head. "I won't say another word."

"We'll find him with or without your help," Blade said, walking to Hickok's side. Kneeling, he gently shook the gunfighter's left shoulder. "Nathan, get up."

Slowly, groaning in pain, Hickok opened his eyes and

gazed in confusion at his surroundings. "Where am I, pard?"

"In Morlock's castle, remember?"

The mention of the madman sufficed to bring Hickok around. "Yeah," he said, sitting up and touching his temple. "Where the heck is the tin man who clobbered me?"

"It was Elphinstone, and he's out cold," Blade said, pointing at the unconscious brute.

The gunfighter spied the Blackfoot's prone form. His eyes widened, and he scrambled over on his hands and knees. "Geronimo!" He looked anxiously at Blade. "Is he hurt bad?"

"No. He should wake up shortly."

Hickok glared at Elphinstone. "I get first dibs on gorilla puss."

Endora stepped in front of her brother, put her hands on her hips and adopted a stance like a protective hen. "You're not to touch a hair on his head."

"Don't fret none, lady. His hair will still be in one piece when I'm done with him."

"We didn't ask you to come here," Endora said, incensed. "Why can't you go away and leave us alone?"

"You already know the reason," Blade said. "We can't turn our backs on the serfs and overlook all the atrocities your family has committed. We'd never be able to live with ourselves. And your family will never let us leave in peace, anyway." He paused. "What happens next is inevitable."

"Nothing is inevitable."

"You're wrong. It's inevitable that all of us must live with the consequences of our acts, and the Morlock clan is long overdue to reap the results of decades of tyranny and savagery."

Endora cocked her head. "How old are you?"

"Sixteen. Why?"

"You must be older than that."

"Don't let his fancy words fool you, lady," Hickok interjected. "He talks that way every now and then, usually after he gets through readin' one of those books by the Greek guy who ran around dressed in a towel."

Geronimo moaned, and his eyelids fluttered. "Nathan?"

"Right here, pard," Hickok said, leaning over his friend.

"That's what I was afraid of."

"Another cut. That's two I owe you."

The Blackfoot's eyes opened, and he struggled to sit up, still woozy from the blow. "Where's the—" he began, then saw their attacker lying on the floor. "What happened?"

"The big guy took the tin man down. Elphinstone is the one wearin' the armor."

"Let's find something we can use to tie him up," Blade proposed, surveying the room.

"I won't let you," Endora stated.

"You can't stop us," Blade said. "And we're not leaving him loose to sneak up on us when our backs are turned."

"I'll keep him right here."

"Not good enough, Endora. We can't trust you, either."

"Then why don't you tie me up, too?" she asked scornfully.

"We will."

The patter of dozens of feet filled the corridor, accompanied by much giggling and tittering. A general commotion ensued with pale figures jostling to see who would stand the nearest to the doorway.

"It's the wimps again," Hickok remarked. "What the dickens do they want now?"

"Oh, outers!" came a high-pitched taunt from a pale

throat. "Come out and play with us, won't you please?"

"Yeah," chimed in another. "All of us are here to play pincushion, and this time you won't scare any of us away. So be nice and come out and die."

CHAPTER NINETEEN

Blade stepped to the doorway and saw dozens of smiling serfs packing the corridor, blocking any possible escape. Every one carried a knife. None made a move to harm him—yet.

"Hello, Pard."

The youth glanced to the right and recognized a pair of friendly, beaming faces. "Tabitha. Selwyn. Not you, too?"

"What do you mean, sir?" Tabitha responded. "We like to play pincushion as much as everyone else."

"But pincushion isn't a game. All of you could be killed."

Tabitha chuckled. "Not us, sir. Why, unless we're eaten or chopped into itty-bitty bits, we just curl into little balls for a couple of hours and wake up as good as new."

The full extent of her insanity staggered Blade. He sadly shook his head and scanned the rows of fragile, thin figures. "You don't understand about dying. You don't know the first thing about pain and suffering, Please,

please, put down your knives and go have fun in the forest."

"But we can't sir," Selwyn said. "The great mast wants us to play pincushion with you, and that's what we must do."

"What if my friends and I don't want to play?"

"You must, sir."

"We don't want to hurt you."

The serfs laughed, exchanging amused looks, and then, all at once and all together, without a signal to spur them forward, they attacked.

A glittering knife almost ripped Blade's left arm open as he stepped backwards and tried to shut the door. Fists and blades rained down upon the wood, and the press of bodies kept the door a foot from the jamb, preventing him from doing more than temporarily thwarting the serfs. Hickok and Geronimo rushed to his aid and added their weight to the fray.

The serfs laughed, giggled and snickered the whole time. As they pounded on the door, as they pushed against the panel in a compact mass, as they slashed at the space between the door and the wall, they did so with the utmost hilarity, and the harder they fought, the more mirth they expressed.

Blade's muscles were taxed to their limits. He pushed on the door until he was red in the face, but after all he'd been through he was in no condition to withstand the combined strength of dozens of determined serfs, no matter how weak they might be individually. Even his finely sculpted physique wasn't made of iron.

"They're gettin' through!" Hickok declared as the door slowly inched inward and the serfs were able to extend their reach.

In the end it was the knives that made Blade acknowledge the door couldn't be held. A razor edge sliced into his left forearm, not much more than a prick, but he realized it was only a matter of time before they inflicted a grievous wound. "On the count of three," he told his companions. "We let go and fall back. Spread out and take as many with you as you can."

"I don't much cotton to gunnin' nymphs," Hickok grunted.

"It's either them or us. We can't afford to go easy on them or we'll never see the Home again."

Standing near Elphinstone, Endora Morlock cackled and mocked them. "You're not so tough now, are you, boys? In a few minutes you'll be lying on the floor, and I'll be dancing in your blood."

"One," Blade said, ignoring the barbs. To think he'd once felt sorry for her!

The nonstop drumming on the door continued, mingling with the laughter and the tittering to create an insane din.

"Two," Blade stated. If nothing else on this trip, he'd learned never to take potential enemies and circumstances at face value. Hidden motives and meanings always lurked beneath the surface, and they had to be diligently peeled off like the layers of a rotten onion to expose the putrid core within.

"Kill them, my little darlings!" Endora cried. "Show them how foolish they were to cross the Morlocks."

"Three," Blade barked and leaned backwards. He held the Marlin in his right hand, leveling the barrel as his friends swiftly backed up and the door crashed inward.

Serfs jammed the doorway in their eagerness to plunge their knives into the youths, beaming inanely, bloodlust animating their eyes.

The Marlin boomed, and two serfs dropped. Blade fired twice more, wishing there was some other way he could stop them, overcome with guilt.

Geronimo's Winchester cracked five times in succession, and with each shot a pale, smirking fury fell.

"Kill them! Kill them!" Endora shrieked.

Doing their best to accommodate her, the serfs pressed inside without a spare glance at their fallen comrades. They were about to crest into the room like a tidal wave breaking on a shore when a lean youth in buckskins barred their path.

Hickok had held himself in reserve for just this moment. A lopsided grin creased his lips as he slapped leather, both Colts clearing leather in a streak of movement too fast for the eye to follow. He thumbed off two shots and bored two slugs through two atrophied brains.

The serfs concentrated their attack on the gunfighter. A male lunged with his knife extended.

Unflinching, Hickok sent a round into the male's nose, then shifted and blasted two others. More took their place, and he gunned them down, a single shot apiece, invariably going for a head shot, firing until both revolvers were empty and a pile of corpses choked the doorway.

Over the pile came the rest of the serfs, their enthusiasm bordering on fanaticism, those in the front laughing the hardest.

Blade saw the gunfighter trying to reload, and he grabbed Hickok's shirt and propelled him backward. Discarding the Marlin, he drew his Bowies and advanced to meet the serfs head-on. Suddenly they were swirling around him, cutting and hacking and cackling, always cackling, thoroughly enjoying themselves. He blocked and countered and stabbed, matching their madness with a frenzy of sheer desperation, becoming a tornado of whirling limbs and flashing Bowies, only dimly aware of Geronimo battling on his right, of the twin tomahawks weaving a lethal tapestry to rival his own.

Incredibly quick, the serfs fought like spitfires, prancing and lancing and thrusting and dancing, always in motion, always laughing.

Fury seized Blade, a fury at these creatures—for they could hardly be called human—who had no regard for life, their own or anyone else's. All that mattered to them was fun, fun, fun, having a good time at the expense of everyone and everything. Work became a game. Killing became a game. Existence was a giant game presided over by an insane games master.

His flesh was pierced and gashed and nicked, but he fought on. His arms flagged and his legs complained, but he endured. The sight of so much blood and gore sickened him, but he let self-preservation take its course and took on all comers.

After a while individual foes no longer existed. In their place was a pale demon of many guises who cackled and popped up here, there and anywhere, wounding him in a score of spots, decorating his clothing with crimson streamers. He killed and killed, and still they came on.

Blade ripped a male from gut to sternum, then severed a woman's neck with a single swipe. He deflected an overhand swing and gave a thrust to the throat in return. A knife bit into his side and he bit back. On and on the combat raged, until all of a sudden he found himself standing alone with a carpet of corpses all about him.

"We did it, pard."

The weary voice drew Blade's attention to the right, where Geronimo and Hickok were back to back, the Blackfoot holding gore-spattered tomahawks, the gunfighter a red-stained axe. Bodies ringed them.

There wasn't a serf alive. They were sprawled in all manner of positions, many coated with blood, ripped and torn and cleaved. And every one, every male and every female, smiled even in death, as if they had played a monumental joke on their slayers, a joke only they comprehended.

"Dear Spirit," Geronimo said softly, "is this what it's really like to be a Warrior? Is this the price we'll pay for protecting our loved ones?"

"I am a mite tuckered out," Hickok confessed.

Blade swallowed and surveyed the slaughter. He spotted Tabitha and Selwyn a few feet to his left, dead side by side, and realized, in horror, that he must have slain them.

"Thank goodness there wasn't any more of those rascals," Hickok said. "A few more minutes and we would have bit the dust."

"I wonder if I should become a Warrior?" Geronimo asked, a question meant more for himself than his friends.

Blade looked down at the wounds he'd sustained and the blood seeping out. One knife had cut his vest right above the heart but missed the skin. His cuts weren't life-threatening, but they hurt terribly.

"You murdered our babies, you fiends!"

The youths turned to find Endora Morlock gazing in shock at the serfs.

"You bastards will suffer for this!" Endora raged. "I'll torture you personally."

"Shut your face, bimbo," Hickok snapped, dropping the axe. He began reloading both Colts.

Endora stepped over several bodies and shook her fists at all three of them. "Why couldn't you leave us alone? We were perfectly happy until you butted in. You barged into our castle, sat in judgment on our lives and decided we were evil, decided you had to meddle in our personal affairs." She trembled in her fury. "You had no right."

Blade licked his dry lips and tasted blood on the tip of his tongue. "We had every right. Evil must be exterminated wherever it's found."

"Who the hell are you to say what's evil and what isn't?"

It was Hickok who answered. "We're Warriors, lady."

"And what is that supposed to mean?"

"It means we know the difference between loving, decent folks and perverts who go around preyin' on people who can't defend themselves. It means you can have one minute to make your peace with your Master."

Both Blade and Geronimo glanced at the gunfighter. "Don't," the giant said.

Endora Morlock snorted in contempt. "My Maker? There is no God, you fool. We are what we are, and that's all there is to it."

Hickok nodded once. "And I'm a Warrior." His right hand swept straight out.

"No!" Blade cried, taking a stride toward him.

The weapons room thundered to the retort of another gunshot, and the lady in white sprouted a hole between her eyes, eyes that conveyed a flicker of astonishment a millisecond before she spun in a graceful pirouette and sank to the floor.

Geronimo dashed over to her and uselessly felt for a pulse. "She's dead."

"What did you expect?" Hickok asked.

"We had no right to kill her," Geronimo said. "How could you, Nathan?"

"Piece of cake," the gunfighter replied. "And we had every right to kill her. She wanted us dead, didn't she? She was goadin' the nymphs on to tear us apart."

"But Warriors aren't supposed to be cold-blooded killers."

"And what do you think Warriors do for a living? Grow flowers? We're trained to kill. That's our purpose in life. Oh, I know we do it to protect the Family and the Home, but when you get down to the nitty-gritty, we kill scumbags for a living."

"There's more to being a Warrior than that," Blade said, staring at Endora's oddly composed features.

"Like what, pard?"

"Like adhering to higher ideals of duty and purpose."

"You've been listenin' to Plato again. Ideals are fine and all, but when those nymphs came through the door at us I'll bet you didn't spend one second thinkin' about ideals, duty and purpose. All you were thinkin' about was stayin' alive and killin' as many of those crazies as you could. Am I right?"

"Of course, but—"

"I rest my case."

"You didn't let me finish. Yes, we kill for a living, but only when the need arises. We can't go around blowing people away for the hell of it. There must be a reason."

"How about savin' the lives of lots of innocent folks? Is that a good enough reason for you? The Morlocks have been torturin' and murderin' people for years. All we're doing is puttin' a stop to it."

Blade dropped the subject. He knew better than to waste his breath trying to persuade the gunfighter to change his mind. Also, the sentiments Hickok expressed matched his own in many respects, but he still disliked the callous way in which Hickok had slain Endora Morlock. It had beem more like an execution than a necessary act of preservation.

"Let's go find the brains of this outfit," Hickok suggested, walking toward the doorway, carefully stepping over the many bodies in his path.

Blade and Geronimo started to follow him.

Unexpectedly, Elphinstone sat up, the armor rasping loudly, then heaved himself erect and surveyed the room. His gaze lingered on the dead serfs and finally on his sister. "Endora?"

The three youths simply watched as the brute sank to his knees and lifted Endora's head into his metal lap.

"Sissie? Talk to Elphie."

Blade could barely stand the sight. Shame saddened his soul, and his broad shoulders slumped dejectedly. Should they just leave Elphinstone to his misery? If they did, he might come after them. Perhaps it would be best to reason with him. "Elphinstone?"

Those dull eyes snapped up, peering through the dented visor, and locked on the youths. "You!" he growled. "You did this to her!"

"Please, Elphinstone," Blade said. "Stay calm."

"Kill!" the brute bellowed, surging to his feet, his sister's head hitting the floor with a thud. "Kill!" he repeated, raising his enormous fists, and charged.

CHAPTER TWENTY

Blade had the Marlin halfway to his shoulders when Geronimo's Winchester cracked twice.

Both rounds were aimed at the visor, one of them flattening against the metal with a distinct ping and not quite penetrating while the second went through the right eye slot, bored through the brute's brain, and pinged a second time when it struck the back of the helmet.

Elphinstone halted, his arms sagged, and he swayed. Although his brain had ceased to function, his body hadn't quite gotten the message. His fingers twitched, as if he wanted to grab something, and his left knee jerked forward as if about to intitiate another step. Then, like a towering tree in the forest, he toppled with a tremendous crash.

"Two down and two to go," Hickok said, departing without a backward glance.

Geronimo slowly lowered the rifle and looked at Blade. "I didn't want to do that."

"I know."

"There was no other choice."

"I know."

"I don't think being a Warrior is all it's cracked up to be."

Blade wheeled and stepped into the corridor where the gunfighter was waiting. "Endora mentioned something about a control room. If we find it, we'll find Morlock."

"A control room for what?"

"I don't know."

A reserved Geronimo joined them and fed new bullets into the Winchester. "Let's get this over with as quickly as possible."

"What's the matter, pard?"

"I may not become a Warrior."

Hickok's mouth dropped. "Why not?"

"I'm not like you, Nathan. When I kill someone, I feel a hurt inside."

"And you think I don't?" Hickok responded, his tone betraying bitterness. "I feel it too, but I don't let it get to me. I control it. I tell myself it has to be done." He turned and walked toward the stairs.

"Nathan?" Blade said.

"What?"

"Why did you shoot her?"

"One of us had to do the job, and it might as well have been me," Hickok said and kept walking.

Blade glanced at Geronimo, whose melancholy visibly intensified. "He did it so we wouldn't have to," he stated in a whisper.

"Me and my big mouth," Geronimo remarked.

They hurried to catch up, and the three of them were soon climbing the steps to the next floor. There were no candles lit, no sounds indicating any of the rooms were occupied, so on they went to the next level, and the floor after that, until eventually they reached the uppermost one, ten stories above the ground. An arched, open window gave them a view of the glittering stars and the inky expanse of countryside and explained the breeze they always felt on the stairway.

A sole candle burned next to a partly open door along the left-hand corridor.

"He's mine," Hickok said, leveling both Colts and stalking forward to the door. He kicked it open and darted inside.

Blade and Geronimo were right on his heels. The giant marveled at a large chamber illuminated by two lanterns that revealed banks of electronic equipment aligned along all four walls. There was no sign of Angus Morlock.

"The crud has skipped," Hickok guessed.

"What is all this?" Geronimo asked, moving to a console and studying a series of switches and knobs.

When Blade noticed a dozen blank squares of glass arranged in three rows on the far wall, curiosity impelled him closer to study them. Their shape prompted vague memories of photographs he'd once seen in a book in the Family library, but he couldn't put his mental finger on the exact photos. Two knobs were positioned under each square.

Hickok walked to a piece of equipment and flicked several toggle switches. "I wonder what these do?"

"Maybe we shouldn't touch anything," Geronimo said. "Morlock might have this room booby-trapped."

"No way, pard. He wouldn't want to damage all this stuff," Hickok said and worked another toggle.

Suddenly, from a speaker mounted on the north wall, came the sound of leaves being stirred by a stronge breeze, the distant wail of a coyote and the croaking of tree frogs.

"Where the blazes is that coming from?"

"Outside somewhere," Geronimo said. "But how?"

An answer formed unbidden in Blade's mind, and with it came comprehension. "A microphone."

"What?" Hickok said.

"A microphone. It's a device that can hear sounds and relay them elsewhere. There must be a mike planted outside the castle walls connected to this room by an underground wire, or else the equipment in here operates on battery power."

"How do you know all this?" Hickok asked.

"I remember reading a book about the electronic age, as it was called, and all the wonderful devices available before the Big Blast. The people had devices for playing music, washing clothes and cooking food in a minute flat," Blade said, indicating the blank squares of glass. "And unless I miss my guess, these are monitors used to keep watch on the grounds." He twisted one of the dials.

A screen in the upper row crackled to life and showed one of the gloomy underground passageways.

"See what I mean," Blade said.

"But how could this gear work after so many years?" Geronimo wondered. "Electricity is a thing of the past."

"Not if the Morlocks have a stockpile of rechargeable batteries," Blade said. At least he understood how Morlock had known he entered the castle from the mausoleum.

"Keep turnin' those dials," Hickok advised.

Blade did so, going from monitor to monitor, and one by one corridors and rooms were dimly depicted, all empty. When there were only three screens left, the weapons room materialized with its grisly carpet of pale, grinning corpses.

"Morlock must have seen the whole thing," Geronimo said.

Blade twisted the second to last dial, revealing yet another corridor, and was disappointed at not finding Morlock. Where was the madman? From the number of monitors, he concluded only the main corridors and some of the rooms were part of the surveillance network. There weren't enough to cover the entire castle. "If the runt saw the whole thing, why didn't he try to help the serfs or sic his walkin' fur rug on us?" Hickok brought up.

"He probably believed we'd be no match for the serfs," Blade guessed. "And I doubt he expected us to kill Endora and Elphinstone. Like Endora said, he's been taking us too lightly all along."

"His mistake," Hickok said.

Blade twirled the last dial and stiffened.

The last scene depicted was the roof. And there, standing on a rampart and staring grimly directly into the camera, stood Angus Morlock with a shotgun cradled in the crook of his left arm. Somehow, he knew he was being observed because he nodded and made a beckoning motion with his right hand.

"He wants us to go up there," Geronimo said.

"Let's not disappoint the crumb," the gunfighter stated.

Blade didn't like the setup one bit. Why would Morlock blatantly challenge them to go onto the roof unless it was a trap?

"Are you comin?" Hickok asked, moving to the door.

"Yeah," Blade said. He stared at the monitor for a few seconds, then went into the passageway with his friends.

"The stairs stop on this floor," Geronimo noted. "There must be another way up."

"Each of us will take a door," Blade directed.

The youths separated. There were seven doors all tolled and it wasn't until Geronimo opened the fifth one and called out, "Here it is!" that they found a spiral metal staircase to the top.

"Well, this is it," Hickok said, inspecting the chambers in his revolvers to be sure the guns were fully loaded.

"I'll go first," Blade volunteered.

"Be my guest," Geronimo said.

Blade went up a step at a time, tilting his neck so he could cover a wide door above. Once there, he tested the knob, found it rotated easily, and looked over his right shoulder. "Are you ready?"

"I was born ready," Hickok said.

"No, but go ahead anyway," Geronimo said.

Tensing, Blade flung the door open and threw himself outside to roll on his shoulder and rise to his knee with the Marlin sweeping the flat area before him.

Morlock had vanished.

The central section of the roof was level except for the doorway leading to the spiral staircase, which had been constructed as an isolated, elevated island in the very middle and fronted the northern battlements.

Blade glanced at the top of the door and saw the camera mounted on a sturdy bracket, so he knew Morlock had been within ten feet of the door a minute or two ago.

There were four ramparts connected to four turrets, one at each corner, and those turrets were the only hiding places on the roof.

"He must be in one of those beehive kind of things," Hickok whispered.

"Spread out," Blade said. "We'll check the turret at the northwest corner first." He rose to a crouching posture and advanced warily. A cool breeze caressed his face and brought to his nostrils a peculiar, pungent animal scent unlike any other he knew. He surmised the wind had carried the scent from an animal in the woods below but immediately realized such couldn't be the case. And if the smell didn't come from below or above, then there was only one explanation. The thought made him slow up, and his friends passed on by.

It couldn't be! Blade told himself, staring at the turret in mounting apprehension. He would have smelled it before now, wouldn't he?

Hickok was the closest to the three steps leading from the rampart into the shadowed turret. Both Colts were out and ready.

Blade moved forward, chiding himself for letting his imagination get the better of him. The thing was in the forest. Had to be.

The gunfighter had two yards to cover when a blood-curdling roar rent the night and the monster squeezed through the turret entrance, all ten feet of hair and muscle and unbridled ferocity.

"Grell!" Geronimo yelled.

Hickok squeezed off four shots so fast they sounded like one. But none stopped the gargantuan mutation. He was lifting his arms to fire at the beast's eyes when a swipe of a brawny arm sent him flying over five yards to crash onto his back, dazed.

"Try me," Geronimo bellowed, lifting the Winchester. Quick as he was, Grell was quicker, and a second swipe tumbled the Blackfoot head over heels to lie in a stunned heap.

Blade felt his blood turn to ice. He gazed into those hellish red orbs and felt as if his life force was being sucked from his body. Fear—total, dominating, terrifying—rooted him in place. He wanted to shoot, but couldn't make his hands move.

Grell snarled and lumbered toward the youth.

A tidal wave of panic engulfed the youth. Never had he been so outright scared. His dearest friends were down, perhaps severely injured and needing his help, and yet he couldn't get his limbs to cooperate with his mind. He saw Grell's long white fangs exposed and Grell's right claw sweeping at his head, and he reacted automatically, spinning and running toward the safety of the doorway and the stairwell, his heart pounding, thinking only of escaping with his life. His spine tingled, and he shivered as he ran.

Somewhere, Morlock laughed.

The sound brought Blade up short in midstride, shocked at what he was about to do. He was fleeing, running away, being a coward. Worse, he was deserting his two best friends, leaving them to suffer a horrible fate at the hands of the madman or the mutation. Tremendous revulsion welled up within him, revulsion at his own behavior. He spun.

Grell had halted and coldly regarded the youth.

How could he be so base, so spineless? Blade asked himself. He'd let instinctive fear get the better of him, but fear could only maintain its grip if the person afraid allowed it to dominate their being. And he wasn't about to have fear override his personality, have it supplant his will. He was a *man,* damn it, a man endowed with the power of choice. He could choose to let instinct win, or he would exercise his free will to do what had to be done.

At that moment, as he stood there confronting the monstrous, growling beast looming above him, he came to grips with his innermost being. His spiritual inheritance triumphed over his animal heritage and in the process forged a soul tempered in the adversity of supreme danger.

Blade smiled.

"Kill him, Grell!" came a shout from the darkness, and the creature stalked forward.

Whipping the Marlin up, Blade went to fire, then paused. No. He wouldn't take the easy way out. If he wanted to truly conquer fear, he must face it fully. The triumph must be total—spirit, mind and body. He threw the rifle to the roof and drew his Bowies.

Grell lifted his massive arms and snarled hideously.

Blade ran straight at the mutation and leaped into the air, his back arched, his hands overhead, the big Bowies held with the blades pointed downward. At the apex of his leap he was only a foot from Grell's head. He could almost feel those baleful red orbs boring into his brain and smelled the beast's fetid breath. For an instant panic tried to reassert control, until he grit his teeth, tensed his steely sinews and swept both knives in a flashing arc, burying a Bowie in each crimson eye, sinking the sharp blades all the way to the hilts.

Grell stiffened, roared and swung his arms, catching the youth a glancing blow that knocked him aside. He staggered backwards, clutching at the Bowies and snarling, and managed to yank both knives out.

Blade gasped when his left side smacked into the hard

stone roof, and he lay still for a few seconds, recovering, then pushed to his feet and dashed to where he'd thrown the rifle. He'd proven his courage to his satisfaction. There was nothing to be gained by further heroics. And without a weapon, slaying the monster would be impossible. He scooped up the Marlin and aimed at the thing's head.

"Put down the gun."

The youth froze at the gravelly command.

"You heard me. Put down the gun, and do it real slow."

Blade estimated Morlock was not more than ten feet to his left and slightly behind him, just out of the line of vision. He could try to nail the madman, but even if he hit Morlock the shotgun might go off, and at such close range it would blow him in half. Reluctantly, he lowered the Marlin.

"Good. Now turn around, boy. I want to see your face when I kill you."

Blade complied, his arms at his sides.

A malicious grin curled Angus Morlock's lips. "At last I have you right where I want you. Any last words?"

The youth refused to give the madman the satisfaction.

"Very well. But I want you to know how much I hate you for what you've done. My daughter and my son, both dead. Poor little Grell, blinded for life. And why? All because I didn't have you slain right away instead of toying with you."

The scraping of calloused soles on the stone surface made Blade twist his head slightly so he could see the mutation. Grell was shuffling toward him, those hairy hands pressed over his ruptured eyes, hissing like an enraged viper.

Morlock glanced at his pet. "Look at him," he said morosely. "Look at what you've done."

Blade shifted, saw that he stood directly between the pet and its master, and instantly took the initiative. "You bloodthirsty brute!'' he shouted. ''You deserve to die!''

Grell lowered his arms, roared again and charged wildly in the direction of the youth's voice.

''What are you doing?'' Morlock exclaimed.

In three great bounds the monster was almost upon Blade. He dived to the right and felt the creature's side brush his legs as it went past, glancing at the madman as he did.

Angus Morlock comprehended the ruse too late. ''No, Grell!'' he yelled, but his pet paid no heed. He already had the shotgun leveled, and he fired into the mutation's chest. The explosive impact stopped Grell for just a moment, and then the beast's swinging hands fell on Morlock's shoulders.

''No!'' the madman screeched. ''It's me, you dumb animal.''

Blade would never know whether Grell recognized the voice of his master. He saw those immense fingers wrap around Morlock's head even as Morlock struggled and bellowed frantically. He saw Grell wrench sharply to the right, then the left. And he heard the snap, loud and clear.

A moment later yet another unfortunate victim crashed lifeless on top of the true beast of Castle Orm.

CHAPTER TWENTY-ONE

The youths watched the flames lick at the pile of four corpses located on the roof near the north battlement and gazed in silence at the black smoke curling into the bright morning sky.

"It's fitting the Morlocks are being burned together," Geronimo commented thoughtfully.

"How do you figure, pard?" Hickok asked.

"Their destinies were intertwined from the start."

The gunfighter chuckled. "If you say so. But you worry me."

"I do?"

"Yep. You're startin' to sound like the big guy."

Sighing, Geronimo stared at their somber friend. "Are you all right?"

"Fine."

"You sure?"

"Drop the subject."

"What's with you?" Hickok asked. "You should be happy, not down in the dumps. We won, didn't we? We took care of these bozos so they'll never kill another innocent wanderer."

"Did we win?" Blade inquired softly.

"We're still alive, ain't we?"

"And what about the serfs?"

"What about 'em?"

Blade glanced at the doorway, his features profoundly troubled. "What happened to their bodies?"

"Who knows?" Hickok said and shrugged. "There must have been a few off playin' somewhere when we killed the rest, and while we were up on the roof they came and dragged the dead nymphs off."

"We weren't up here long enough for all the bodies to be removed."

"You don't know that for certain,." Hickok said. He stretched and crinkled his nose. "Boy, the Morlocks and that hairy critter aren't exactly roses, if you get my drift. Let's skedaddle. I want to get back to the Home."

They turned and walked to the doorway, two of them deep in contemplation, the third grinning at the fitting conclusion of their adventure. At the doorway all three abruptly halted when they heard the sounds wafting up from far, far below, the sounds of giggling and tittering.

EPILOGUE

Plato closed the file and leaned back in the wooden chair, his brow creased, his blue eyes narrowed, and absently ran his right hand through his long gray beard. An unexpected knock on the cabin door curtailed his reflection. "Come in," he called out.

The door swung inward to reveal a seven-foot giant wearing a black leather vest and green fatigue pants. Around his waist were strapped two Bowies. "Hi, Plato. Sorry to bother you."

"Nonsense, Blade. How may I be of service?"

The giant's eyes strayed to the Family Leader's lap. "The Chronicler told me you have a certain file I need."

"This one?" Plato asked innocently, tapping the blue cover.

"Yeah. Are you done with it?"

"Sure am." Plato said, holding the file out. "Be my guest."

"Thanks." Blade walked over and took it, his gaze lingering on the older man's face. "Any particular reason you were reading this one?"

"No," Plato fibbed.

Blade turned to go. "Well, I'll see you later."

"How is Gabe doing?"

The giant stopped and glanced at his mentor. "You heard, huh?"

"I would imagine everyone in the Family knows the story by now."

Blade frowned. "You're probably right."

"No one blames him for what happened."

"He blames himself."

A kindly chuckle issued from Plato's lips. "When you're five years-old and you see a slavering, mutated black bear bearing down on you, your first reaction is to run. He has nothing to be ashamed of. Especially since, as I understand it, he only ran a dozen yards or so, then went back to get Tommy."

"That's what happened," Blade confirmed. "Tommy was so scared he just stood there. They were both lucky that Ares heard Gabe screaming for Tommy to run and got there in time to kill the mutant."

"So all's well that ends well."

"Not quite. Gabe is upset because he ran in the first place. He thinks he's a coward and can never grow up to become a Warrior like me."

"I take it a bedtime story is in order?"

Blade nodded. "I'm hoping it will help."

"If he's anything like his father—and I know he is—Gabe will recover quickly. We all do when we're that young."

The giant smiled and stepped to the doorway. "Thanks again."

"Say, Blade?"

"Yes?"

"Did anyone ever go back to Castle Orm?"

"No."

"One of these days we should go there."

"One of these days."